MEET THE GIRL TALK CHARACTERS

Sabrina Wells is petite, with curly auburn hair, sparkling hazel eyes, and a bubbly personality. Sabrina loves magazines, shopping, sleepovers, and most of all, she loves talking to her best friends.

Katie Campbell is a straight-A student and super athlete. With her blond hair, blue eyes, and matching clothes, she's everyone's idea of Lttle Miss Perfect. But Katie has a few surprises for everyone, including herself!

Randy Zak has just moved to Acorn Falls from New York City, and is she ever cool! With her radical spiked haircut and her hip New York clothes, Randy teaches everyone just how much fun it is to be different.

Allison Cloud is a Native American Indian. Allison's supersmart and really beautiful. But she has one major problem: She's thirteen years old, five foot seven, and still growing!

CENTER STAGE

By L. E. Blair

GIRL TALK® series created by Western Publishing Company, Inc.

Western Publishing Company, Inc., Racine, Wisconsin 53404

Text by Susan Sloate

Chapter One

"I'm so excited I could just die!" I exclaimed. I was sitting in a big theater in Minneapolis with my best friends, Katie Campbell, Randy Zak, Allison Cloud, and my mom. I knew they were as excited as I was.

"Take it easy, Sabrina," my mom said with a laugh. "You'll bounce right out of your seat before the play even starts!"

My mom had brought us all the way from Acorn Falls, where we live, to see a professional performance of Romeo and Juliet. The curtain was already up. The set looked like an old-time English bar.

"The stage sure looks great," said Randy. Randy's really into scenery and art. She's from New York City, supercool, with spiked black hair and the wildest clothes I've ever seen. Randy especially likes wearing black. Tonight she was wearing a black suede mini-skirt and a

1

black sweatshirt with silver lightning bolts painted on it and silver earrings and bracelets. She looked awesome.

"Remember the play?" Allison asked. "The opening scene takes place in the public streets." Al could see that I was trying to figure out the set. She knows all about Shakespeare — and most other things, too! Al's also incredible-looking. She has beautiful long black hair that she wears in a braid. She's a Native American, one hundred percent Chippewa, and she's the tallest girl in seventh grade at our school — Bradley Junior High. The deep blue dress and vivid blue-and-violet scarf that she wore tonight made her look just like a model.

Katie laughed. "I'll bet Allison knows the whole play word for word," she teased. Katie had her blond hair pinned back with blue barrettes, and, as usual, she looked great.

Katie's clothes are always perfect, too. She wears everything color-coordinated, like my favorite magazine, Young Chic, says you're supposed to. Tonight she was in a pink sweater, pink skirt, white blouse, pink-and-white belt.

Just as Allison started to answer Katie, the lights began to dim. You didn't have to know

Shakespeare to know what that meant! "Hey, guys, it's starting!" I whispered.

I felt like I'd been walking on clouds ever since my mother told me she'd gotten tickets for Romeo and Juliet. It's been my favorite play since we read it English class earlier this year. It's so romantic. I really want to be an actress, so seeing any play is great exposure for me. You never know what tips you may pick up just from watching. Learn to Act at Home, which is a video I've rented a lot this year, says going to the theater is one of the best ways an actress can learn her craft.

The play was about to begin, so I got comfortable in my seat, folding my plaid miniskirt under me. The skirt matched my plaid vest, and I was wearing a bright yellow sweater underneath. I like wearing bright colors. I think they go well with my reddish hair and hazel eyes.

From the minute the Capulets and the Montagues started fighting, I felt like I was in a dream. I could feel myself being drawn in further and further as Romeo and Juliet fell in love.

"Earth to Sabs!" Katie nudged me. "Sabs, wake up!"

3

"Huh? What? Did I miss something?" I asked.

"It's intermission!" Randy practically shouted at me. "Get your head out of the clouds!"

"I'm really thirsty," said Katie.

Randy laughed. "I am, too. It must be from watching all those fight scenes. You know, this is pretty cool stuff."

"I like all the beautiful poetry," Allison added. "It's so sad. Fate is really controlling their lives."

"It's a little like Sabs and her horoscopes," Katie teased me. "She thinks the stars control what happens to us, too."

I giggled. "Well, at least I never read a horoscope that said any of us was going to fall in love with the wrong guy and die over it!" It was true, though, I do love reading horoscopes. They are absolutely right so much of the time that I always think it's worthwhile to check them out. I'd much rather be prepared for my future.

Now that I was out of the spell of the play, I was full of energy. "I'll go for the sodas," I volunteered. "What do you want?"

"Are you sure, Sabrina?" my mom asked. "That's an awful lot to carry by yourself."

"I can handle it, Mom," I assured her.

Allison and Katie asked for cola, Randy for sparkling water. My mom said she'd have coffee. I took my purse and bounded up the aisle. Watching all those actors running around the stage made me want to run around, too!

The line at the refreshment stand was very long, so I knew I'd have to wait a long time. I didn't realize, though, that by the time I got to the head of the line, the play would be about to start again. Quickly I asked for the drinks and handed over the first bill I found in my wallet to pay for them.

The counterman slid over a carton of drinks and my change. I picked up the carton and headed back to our seats.

But the lights dimmed as I walked into the auditorium, and I had trouble finding my way. Everyone was getting very quiet and watching the stage. "Mom?" I whispered as I walked along. "Hey, Katie? Al? Randy?"

"Here," I heard Katie's voice answer. I moved toward her and found my seat.

"Here you go, guys," I whispered, handing over the carton. I must have had way too much in my hands, though, because the carton tipped over and started to fall. To make matters worse, one of the drinks wasn't tightly capped, and it tipped over, too, and splashed all over the floor! Along with most of my change!

"Oh, no!" I heard Randy cry out.

"Sorry, Ran," I whispered.

"No problemo, Sabs," she assured me, grabbing at the napkins I'd brought with me. Naturally, they were soaked.

"Here, Randy," said Katie, handing over some tissues from her purse. Allison gave Randy hers, too. For a while Randy scrubbed at her clothes and I scrounged around for the coins under my seat.

"I think it's all gone," Randy said finally. "I just hope it wasn't mine. I'm still dying of thirst."

I sniffed at the wet tissues she dumped in the carton. "Smells like coffee, I think," I said. "It must have been my mom's."

"They all smell like coffee," said Allison, sniffing at the other containers. "What did you order?"

I couldn't remember exactly. I must have been thinking so hard about Romeo and Juliet that I didn't realize what I was saying. The guy in line in front of me had asked for four coffees. Maybe I just said that I'd have the same thing.

"Maybe next time one of us should go with you," Katie advised.

"I can do it myself, Katie," I answered, a little hurt. "This was just a mistake."

"Yeah, but things have a way of getting out of hand when you do them yourself," Randy said with a giggle.

We all quieted down now, since the play had started up again. I didn't want to miss a word. The minute I looked at the stage, I forgot everything else — the auditorium, the audience, even my friends. All I could think about was poor Juliet and her wonderful, brave Romeo. I felt like nothing else in the world existed!

Chapter Two

I was still in a daze when the play ended, but I clapped like crazy for the actors, especially the actress playing Juliet. She looked lots older than fourteen, which is the age Juliet's supposed to be in the play. So I guess she must have been a really good actress, if she could make us believe she was fourteen.

"You've got that look on your face, Sabrina," Katie said, smiling at me.

"What look?" I wanted to know.

"You know, when you're dreaming about acting. You look like you're imagining yourself right up there onstage."

"Yeah, dressed up like that funny old nurse and creaking around the floor!" Randy added.

I swatted at her with one hand. "I would definitely not creak!"

When we finally stood up to leave, my mom warned us, "It's a long drive back, girls. Anyone want to use the ladies' room?"

"I do," I said. Everybody else was okay, so I headed off alone. I could still see the actors saying their parts and pacing around the stage.

I was so busy thinking about the play that I walked right past the sign for the ladies' room and had to walk back. I pushed open the door and saw a little boy inside, facing me.

"What are you doing here?" he asked. He sounded really annoyed.

I was the one who should be annoyed. What was a boy doing in the girls' rest room, anyway? "Hey, kid, you shouldn't be in here," I told him. "You want the next door down."

"I do not!" he spat at me. "You're the one who's lost."

"I am not!" I said hotly. I couldn't believe that they'd let a boy in the girls' room. No one even seemed to notice the mistake. Maybe his mother was coming in after him.

Just then the door opened and a hand grabbed me. "Let go of me!" I shrieked.

"Come on, Sabs!" Randy said. It was her hand on my shoulder. "You're in the wrong place!"

She pulled me outside and showed me the

sign, which read GENTLEMEN. I could feel my body blush starting. First my face turns red, then I can feel my whole body turn red from my head to my toes. I was really embarrassed!

In the car going home, though, I lapsed right back into thinking about the play. I couldn't seem to stop hearing those great speeches in my head.

"You better make sure Sabs is okay," I heard Katie say. "She hasn't said a word in almost five minutes."

Allison put a hand on my forehead. "She hasn't got a temperature."

"Maybe . . ." Randy pretended to look tragic. "Maybe it's already too late."

Katie nodded. "It is too late. I'm afraid she's . . ." She let out a very convincing sob. ". . . she's stagestruck!" Everyone laughed.

I laughed, too, and tossed my program at them. "Wasn't the play great, guys? Wasn't it just amazing?"

"Almost as good as I Dismember Grandma," Randy agreed. Randy loves horror movies, and she's always trying to get us to watch them with her.

I suddenly had a great idea! "We should do

something like that," I said. "Let's start a seventh-grade drama club. Then we can put on our own shows all the time!"

"That's a terrific idea!" Katie said. "And you're the perfect one to get it started, Sabs."

"That's right," Randy chimed in. "As class president, you can get support from everybody else. They'll love it!"

"We can help, too," Allison offered. "I'll be the stage manager."

"Really?" I asked. I couldn't believe it. I had absolutely the best friends in the world!

"Sure," Randy agreed. "We'll all work behind the scenes. Music, lighting, costumes . . ."

"As long as you don't expect us to act," Katie said. I remembered the time she ended up in the school production of Grease at the very last minute. She was just fabulous, too, but Katie preferred being backstage. "I can make posters and things for publicity, if you want."

"That'd be great!" I said.

Mom swung the car into Katie's driveway. "Here you are, Katie. Good night."

Katie climbed out. "Good night, Mrs. Wells," she called. "Thanks a lot. I'll call you, Sabs. Let's get together tomorrow and start planning!"

We dropped off Randy and Allison at their houses and drove home.

I went up to my bedroom, which is the greatest. It's in the attic. I've got four brothers and being the only girl means I get a bedroom to myself. My room has walls that slope toward the ceiling. It's very private and different-looking.

Tonight, though, I hardly looked at it. All I could think about was how amazing the play had been and how great it would be to be in a drama club! We'd be able to do shows all the time. It was going to be awesome!

Chapter Three

The next afternoon everyone gathered in my kitchen. It was Sunday and we were going to the mall later. But first we wanted to talk about the new seventh-grade drama club. It would have to be all planned out before we told everyone at school about it.

My mom had just finished baking brownies, so we piled a plate full of them. Katie put some popcorn in the microwave. She's over at my house so much that she knows where to find everything she needs.

Naturally, I hadn't intended to eat anything. I was working hard at my self-improvement program. My current project was losing about six pounds. But it was too hard to resist the smells of chocolate and hot popcorn. I dug into the popcorn bowls as soon as they were ready. Popcorn is really low in calories, so it's a good snack food.

We set the food on the table. I got some juice and soda out of the fridge. I took a raspberry seltzer for myself. I'm really getting into seltzers. They're a lot healthier than soda because they don't have all that sugar and stuff.

Katie had her notebook out and was uncapping a pen. "So what's the plan, Sabs?" she asked.

"Well, uh, I . . ." I couldn't think of anything to say. Everybody was looking at me, waiting for me to come up with the ideas. I decided to jump right in. "I want to start a seventh-grade drama club. That way we could do plays all the time."

"Hear, hear!" Randy cheered.

"Great idea!" said Katie. She wrote down "Drama club — seventh grade."

"What play should we start with?" Allison asked.

I had been thinking about that, so I had my answer all ready. "I want to do Romeo and Juliet, just the way we saw it in Minneapolis," I told them. "Won't it be fabulous?" I could already picture my hair flowing over my shoulders and the wonderful costume I could wear as Juliet. I would make a great Juliet. And maybe a really cute boy would play Romeo. I could think of one or two in our class who would make perfect Romeos.

"Sabs!" Randy said. "You can't do Romeo and Juliet!"

"Why not?" I asked.

"None of the kids want to do Shakespeare!" Randy said. She made it sound like Shakespeare was a disease.

Just then the door opened and my twin brother, Sam, burst in, followed by his friends Nick Robbins and Jason McKee. "Whoa, brownies!" Sam whooped. "My favorite!"

He plunged his hand right into the plate of brownies and snatched up about four in one scoop. I couldn't believe it. I didn't think his hand was that big, to begin with. "Sam, could you leave some for us?" I asked.

"Sorry, Sabs," Nick said, snatching at the plate himself.

By now there wasn't a brownie left on the plate. Sam was dipping into the popcorn, and there wasn't much of that left, either.

"Hey, it's cold outside!" Jason said, plunging his hands into the popcorn. He took out the last little handful in the bowl. "We need food to stick to our ribs!"

"Oh, yeah?" Randy said softly. I could see she had an idea. Her eyes were starting to sparkle. Slowly she got up from the table. Her hand, which was full of popcorn, came out from behind her back. "Food that sticks to your ribs? Why didn't you say so?"

In a minute she'd grabbed Jason by his jacket and stuffed her popcorn inside! He yelled as she squished the popcorn right against his chest. "There you go, Jason!" Randy said sweetly. "It should stick to your ribs now!"

Sam and Nick howled with laughter as Jason jumped up and down, trying to get the popcorn out of his shirt. I couldn't help laughing, either. He looked so goofy!

When I got up with my fistful of popcorn, Nick and Sam ducked away fast. In fact, they were all set to run out the door again when Allison said suddenly, "Wait, guys. We need to ask your opinion about something."

I looked at Allison like she was nuts. What could we possibly want to talk to these guys about?

Allison looked very serious as she said, "Sit down. We won't throw anything else at you."

"How could you?" Nick asked. "There isn't

16

anything left." He was right. The plate was empty, except for a few measly brownie crumbs, and there were only unpopped kernels left in the popcorn bowl. The guys obviously figured they were safe from further attack. So they sat down and looked at Allison.

Allison can be a little shy around boys, but after a minute she said, "Sabs has this great idea. She wants to start a seventh-grade drama club."

"And I want to start the first show right away!" I added.

"That is a great idea, Sabs!" Sam agreed. "It's about time we came up with a new project."

Sam always amazes me. He loves to tease me and make me furious, but when the chips are down, he always supports me.

"That sounds cool," Nick said enthusiastically.

"Yeah, it'll be lots of fun," Jason added. "What play are we going to do?"

"That's right," Sam said. "How do we start?"

I stood up tall and gave it to him right between the eyes. "Romeo and Juliet," I said proudly.

There was total silence in the kitchen. Sam looked at Nick, and Nick looked at Jason. Then they looked down at the floor. I could have definitely heard a pin drop.

"Well?" I said. "Isn't that an awesome idea?"

Nick cleared his throat. "Uh . . . Sabrina," he said. "There's, uh, a lot of the kids won't want to do Romeo and Juliet."

"Definitely," Sam jumped in. "It's bad enough we have to read it in class. Who wants to spend time after school with all those 'thees' and 'thous'? I mean, nobody ever says what they mean. It's all this stupid poetry. Who can even understand it?"

"You are so dumb, Sam Wells," I retorted. "Shakespeare's been around for hundreds of years because people like all that poetry and stuff, and . . . and . . ." I made the mistake of looking over at my friends for support.

They didn't look very supportive. Katie was twisting a lock of hair around her pencil, Allison was staring down at the floor, and Randy was looking around at the kitchen walls. Now I know our kitchen's nice, but nobody stares at wallpaper like that. I realized I was in trouble.

The boys realized it, too. "Look at that!" Sam

said. "Even your friends don't like the idea!"

"Cut it out, Sam," Randy said. She sounded sort of unhappy. I could see this idea hadn't exactly grabbed anybody.

Sam, Nick, and Jason left the room very quietly. I suddenly felt very discouraged. Maybe this wasn't the great idea I thought it was. I mean, why would my friends look so depressed about it when they'd been all thrilled just a few minutes ago?

I sat down at the kitchen table. "Maybe it doesn't have to be Romeo and Juliet," I said hesitantly.

Instantly my friends perked up. "Now you're talking!" Randy shouted. "I knew you'd see the light!"

"Which play would you rather do?" Allison asked softly.

I got stuck on that question. "I don't know," I admitted finally. I looked around the table. Nobody else seemed to have any ideas, either. We all just sat around and thought very quietly for a minute.

"I've got an idea," Allison said finally. "Why don't you and I meet in the library tomorrow during free period, Sabs? We'll go through the drama section together."

"That's a great idea, Allison!" Katie agreed. "The library has so many plays, you'll definitely find the right one there!"

"Good idea, Al," I said. "Thanks for helping me."

"A good thing, too," Randy added. "Or we might get stuck with Julius Caesar, or something even creepier!"

Chapter Four

"I made it!" I said breathlessly, plopping down next to Allison in the library.

It was already a few minutes into our free period. I would have been there right on time, but when I had opened the locker I share with Katie to put away my books, a shower of stuff — most of it mine — fell right down on my head! I had to push everything back in and snap the combination lock on before I could meet Allison.

Allison was sitting at a big table, surrounded by a huge pile of books. She was wearing a beautiful sweater with huge roses knitted into the pattern and deep rose stirrup pants. She had an open notebook in front of her and was already writing things down.

"Hi, Sabrina," Allison said. "I'll be done with this list in a sec."

I looked at it. There were already about twelve titles on the list. Allison was reading the title page of a big volume in front of her and writing away. I poked her with my pencil.

"Hey!" I whispered. "How can you know which titles to write down? Some of these plays may be terrible!"

"It's okay," Allison assured me. "I've read these plays. I'm only writing down the ones I think would be fun to do."

I couldn't believe it! I mean, I plan to be an actress and I haven't read as many plays as Allison has! She's really amazing.

I looked over her shoulder at some of the titles: The Man Who Came to Dinner and Harvey and Arsenic and Old Lace. "Hey!" I said. "I don't know any of these!"

"Sh!" hissed the school librarian, Ms. Reed. I hadn't realized I was talking out loud, but when I looked up, it seemed as though everybody in the library was looking in my direction. Quickly I buried my face in the new issue of Young Chic.

I happen to think it was an omen that I opened it to the horoscope page. I hadn't read my horoscope for the month yet, so I was really eager to find out what was in store for me. Soon I found the prediction for Pisces: "Enjoy the scenery of a magical kingdom. It's a long road but you will be surrounded by friends." I looked over at Allison, who was carefully writing down more titles. The part about friends was right, anyway. I just wish I knew what the rest of it meant.

Maybe it was trying to tell me something about the play we should put on? I looked at the titles and nudged Allison. "Are any of those about a road or a kingdom?" I whispered as quietly as I could. I wasn't taking any chances that Ms. Reed would kick us out of the library before we'd finished our research.

Allison looked down at her list. "No . . . most of them are comedies with lots of parts. I thought you might like to do a comedy."

"Can you think of a play about a journey?" I asked. "I think that would be good for us to do."

Allison saw the copy of Young Chic in front of me and sighed. "Horoscopes again?"

"It might be a sign," I explained. "Just keep your eyes open for a play about a journey."

Allison closed the book in front of her and set it on top of a stack of others. Then she opened another one. Clearly, she didn't need me to help read the play titles and write them down. Maybe I could help out in another way. "Are you done with those?" I asked her. "I'll put them back for you."

"That'd be great," Allison answered. "I'll just look through these last ones."

I jumped up and lifted the stack of books. They were really heavy, but if I kept my arms low, I could hold them without too much trouble. In order to keep my balance, I started walking backwards, toward the drama section, with nice slow steps. Suddenly I bumped into something. The books I was carrying fell to the floor with a loud crash!

"Sabrina Wells!" I heard Ms. Reed call after me. "Would you please try to be quiet!"

I turned around to see what I'd bumped into. It was Winslow Barton. He still had his back to me — obviously we had bumped back-to-back. He was tottering around, trying to balance a pretty huge stack of books which were about to slide right down to the floor.

"Sorry, Winslow," I said quickly. "Here, I'll help you." I tried to push the books together for him. But since I'm so short, I couldn't reach high enough. In a second, all the books Winslow was holding were scattered on the floor right next to mine.

Winslow looked at me through his thick, round glasses and sighed. "That's all right, Sabrina," he said. "Don't help me. I'll get them." He knelt down to pick up the books while I just stood there, feeling really stupid.

I looked at his books. Some of them were really babyish, the kind of books I thought Winslow had outgrown long ago. He's the smartest kid in school, practically, and gets these terrific grades in math and science. But the books he had were all fairy tales and children's stories.

"Gee, Winslow," I couldn't help saying, "don't you think you're a little old for this stuff?"

He looked at me very seriously as he picked up the books. "I'm doing a paper for English," he explained. "It's about childhood myths and how they shape our outlook on life."

Leave it to Winslow. Still, I'm glad he wasn't just dying to read Snow White again. He took his books and marched off, and I bent over to pick up the books I'd dropped.

"Isn't that just the cutest thing!" I heard a voice say behind me.

Oh, no. It was Stacy Hansen, better known as

Stacy the Great. That's what Katie, Allison, Randy, and I call her. She's in the seventh grade just like us, but Stacy thinks she's really cool, just because she's the principal's daughter. I always seem to mess up when Stacy's around.

I turned around. There she was, in a deep purple dress and matching bracelets, with her friends B. Z. Latimer, Laurel Spencer, and Eva Malone.

"Isn't that cute?" Stacy asked, as if she didn't know I was listening. "Just happening to run into Winslow like that?"

"You can tell she's crazy about him," Eva added. "I mean, walking backwards into somebody can't be an accident!"

I was getting furious. I hate it when they say things like that. The worst part is, I never seem to be able to think of a good comeback. "It was an accident," I said hotly. "I happen to be doing some very important research here!"

"On what?" Stacy giggled. "The Wizard of Oz?" She looked down at one of the books on the floor.

Oh, no! That must be one of Winslow's. He obviously hadn't noticed he'd left it there. But I wasn't going to try to explain. Stacy didn't deserve it. "As a matter of fact," I said haughtily, "I may just have a few surprises in store for the whole school."

I picked up the rest of the books and started to walk away. I looked down at The Wizard of Oz, which was the top book on my pile. I remembered how much I'd always loved the movie. Suddenly I had the most awesome idea!

"Allison!" I hurried over to her table, where she was still writing in her notebook. "I've got it! I know the perfect first play for the seventh-grade drama club!"

Allison looked up. "What is it?" she asked.

"The Wizard of Oz!" I shouted triumphantly, holding out the book. "A play of the movie! With all the songs and dances and everything!"

"Sabrina Wells!" Ms. Reed said sharply. "Will you please keep your voice down!"

"We'd better get out of here," Allison advised. We checked out the book and hurried out of the library and into the hallway.

"It's the perfect play!" I said. I was so excited, I was jumping up and down. "Everybody knows the movie and the songs! They'll love it!"

"It would be great," Allison said thoughtfully. "And there's all kinds of neat lights and sets and stuff. It would even be fun for the technical crews to work on."

I was so thrilled I wanted to laugh out loud. It was too perfect! "It even fits in with my horoscope!" I said. "A magical kingdom, a journey, surrounded by friends . . . that's what happens to Dorothy!" Obviously this also meant I was destined to play the leading role which was something I really, really wanted to do. Things just couldn't be working out better!

Allison laughed. "Sometimes, Sabrina, it does seem like something mystical is guiding your footsteps."

She was right. I could just see our play coming to life, right here at Bradley. It was going to be the best play ever!

Chapter Five

That afternoon, after school, I had an appointment to see Mr. Hansen, the principal at Bradley Junior High, to ask him to let us start a drama club. I had picked a special outfit—something I hoped would make me look very responsible. I was wearing a dark green skirt with a light-green-and-black sweater over it. I borrowed this great a silver drama brooch my mom has and pinned it on. It had the masks of comedy and tragedy next to each other. I figured it was appropriate since we'd be talking about the the theater.

Practically the first thing I heard, waiting in the principal's office, was "Nice pin, Sabrina." I looked over. Oh, no! There were Eva and Laurel, giggling in the corner. I glared at them. Eva sneered at the comedy and tragedy masks. "What's the matter? Can't make up your mind if you're happy or depressed?"

For once I thought of exactly the right come-back. "No problem," I shot back. "Whenever I see you, it's no contest. Deep depression!"

"Funny, very funny," Eva said sarcastically. "I bet it took you all night to come up with that one."

Before I could answer, the door to Mr. Hansen's office opened, and Stacy the Great came out, wearing a shiny silver tunic and black pants. I had to admit she looked good, with her blond hair swinging over her shoulder.

Stacy saw me waiting and immediately flipped her hair back. "Thank you, Daddy," she said in her sweetest-sugar tone. "I'll see you at dinner."

I almost gagged. Everyone knows Stacy is the principal's daughter, but sometimes the way she plays it up is beyond sickening.

"Hello, Sabrina," Mr. Hansen said, smiling at me from his office door. He has the same phony smile that Stacy does. I guess that's where she gets it from. "Won't you come in now?"

I forgot all about Stacy as I walked into Mr. Hansen's office.

"What can I do for you, Sabrina?" Mr. Hansen asked, sitting down at his big desk. "You mentioned yesterday that you have a project to propose for the seventh grade."

I took a deep breath. "Yes, Mr. Hansen. You see, I saw this play in Minneapolis over the weekend." I explained about Romeo and Juliet and how great it was and how we wanted to start a seventh-grade drama club at Bradley. I told him all about my idea for The Wizard of Oz.

"Well, that's certainly very ambitious," Mr. Hansen said when I'd finished. "Put it on yourselves, hm? And I guess you'll be directing it yourself?"

I opened my mouth to speak, then closed it again. Direct it? A whole play? I had never thought of that. Of course, I wanted to play Dorothy, but it never occurred to me that I'd get involved with telling everybody what to do.

On the other hand, it was a perfect opportunity. I'd be getting some really valuable stage experience. It could only help my acting career!

"Absolutely," I said boldly. "I'll be directing it."

"Well, well, that's fine. I think you've got a wonderful idea there, Sabrina. Now, a few questions. Have you thought about how the club will be structured? Have you spoken to anyone about being a faculty adviser? And when do you see this show opening?"

I couldn't believe I was sitting with the principal of Bradley Junior High, talking about opening nights and dates for rehearsals and everything. I felt like a real grown-up. And Mr. Hansen was actually treating me like one, too! I guess when you suddenly take on a lot of responsibility, it really impresses adults.

A little later, when we'd agreed on the final details, Mr. Hansen actually shook hands with me. "Good luck!" he said heartily. "I'll be looking forward to seeing the play." As I walked out the door, I could hear him actually whistling "We're Off to See the Wizard." I had it made!

"He loved it!" I reported to my friends. They were waiting for me at Fitzie's. Fitzie's is this great ice-cream parlor where we hang out. "We're all set on rehearsal dates and opening night and everything! We're now an official club. All we have to do is hold a planning meeting."

"That's fantastic, Sabs!" Randy exclaimed. "That means we can get started right away!" Randy was wearing the neatest hat I've ever seen. It was a biker's cap studded with silver and it had at least a dozen funny little buttons pinned all over it.

"Who's the faculty adviser going to be?" asked Katie. "Did you talk about that?"

"Yes," I answered. "Mr. Hansen suggested asking Mr. Metcalf, so I'll talk to him tomorrow after class."

"What are the dates you decided on?" Allison asked. She was munching on a salad.

I consulted my notepad. "Well, we start rehearsals next week," I told them. "And we open in less than four weeks."

"Wow! That doesn't give us much time!" Katie said. "We'd better get into casting and rehearsals right away."

"And props and lights and sets," Randy chimed in. "We should figure out exactly what props we're going to need, so we can start rounding those up."

"Good idea, Randy," Katie agreed. "Let's see, what do we need for The Wizard of Oz?"

We all sat thinking about it. I was concentrating so hard, I hardly tasted my chocolate yogurt shake. Katie opened her notebook to write down our ideas.

"Okay, guys, let's just talk about props for right now," Randy told us. "We can probably borrow or make costumes, so that won't be a problem. But the props —"

"A broomstick for the witch!" Katie suggested. "That's what Dorothy and her friends have to fetch for the Wizard."

"No problem. I'll borrow our broom from home," Randy said confidently. "What else?"

"A basket for Dorothy to carry," Allison spoke up. "That's what she puts Toto in!"

"We've got a picnic basket at home," Katie said. "It's small enough for somebody to loop over her arm." She winked at me as she said it. I had a funny feeling Katie already knew that I wanted to play Dorothy myself.

"A bicycle for Miss Gulch!" I said. "And the diploma and stuff the Wizard gives the Scarecrow, the Lion, and the Tin Man!"

Allison wrote as fast as she could, with all of us shouting out suggestions. "Oh!" I said finally, remembering something important. "Wait a minute. The ruby slippers — they're the biggest prop of all!"

"Where are we going to get those?" Katie asked.

There was a silence as we all thought. I knew that none of us owned a pair of shoes like the ruby slippers Judy Garland wore in the movie. And somehow I felt very sure that unless the slippers were just exactly right, the show would never come off the way I wanted it to.

Just then Sam and his pals came over to our booth and squeezed in next to us.

"I hear the drama club's going to put on The Wizard of Oz!" Sam said excitedly. "Now, that's a cool idea for a show! When are we going to have our first meeting?"

I stared at him. "How did you know we're doing The Wizard of Oz?" I asked. Could he read my mind long distance? This was really weird.

"Stacy told him," Jason explained.

"Why, that little sneak!" Randy exclaimed. "She must have listened through the door while you talked to Mr. Hansen!"

Speak of the devil, and here she was. The next thing I knew, Stacy and her clones were strolling toward our booth.

"I hear you're going to try to put on The Wizard of Oz," Stacy remarked. "I certainly hope you'll be fair in casting it."

I couldn't believe it! "Of course I will be," I said indignantly. "Whoever joins the club can be in the play."

"Oh, I don't want to join your silly club," Stacy said with a sneer. "You'll just have to hold open auditions."

Now that made me mad. What was so bad about our club? Stacy just couldn't bear the idea of a good idea coming from somebody else, or of joining a group where she wasn't the leader. I knew I shouldn't let her get to me, but she had really hurt my feelings this time.

I stood up with as much dignity as I possibly could and pointed to my glass. "Stacy," I said in my sweetest tone, "if you don't want to join the drama club, then this chocolate shake has a better chance of getting into The Wizard of Oz than you do!"

Stacy looked furious. then she spun around in a swirl of silver and stormed out of Fitzie's She didn't even stop to make a comeback. I really hoped she wouldn't make more trouble for the drama club.

Chapter Six

The next morning was Tuesday. I stood next to Mr. Hansen while he broadcast his announcements over the P.A. system. Katie and I had worked for hours the night before on an announcement for me to read in front of the school. I was a little nervous, but she'd insisted I read it over the phone to her until I had it down perfectly.

Mr. Hansen finished his announcements, then cleared his throat. "Will you now please give your undivided attention to Sabrina Wells, seventh-grade class president, who has a special announcement for the seventh grade. Sabrina?"

He motioned me to step in front of the microphone. I hadn't been that nervous before, but suddenly I could feel my whole throat tightening up. It was like somebody had their hand on me and was squeezing tighter and tighter. I could hardly breathe, and I wasn't sure I'd even be able to get the words out of my mouth. But I smiled at Mr. Hansen and walked to the microphone.

"This announcement . . ." Oh, no! I couldn't believe it! My voice was so out of control that it had gone up at least an octave. I sounded like one of the Munchkins!

I cleared my throat and tried again. "This announcement . . ." I still sounded like a Munchkin. Mr. Hansen motioned for me to continue, but I was afraid to open my mouth.

Mr. Hansen saw me hesitate in front of the microphone. He made a breathing motion and gestured to me to take some deep breaths. I did, and suddenly it felt like the hand on my throat was gone.

I took another deep breath and opened my mouth once more. "I am making this announcement to introduce the new seventh-grade drama club! Our premiere production will be The Wizard of Oz!" I said. Ohmygosh! I'd spoken so loudly, the microphone was vibrating! I immediately lowered my voice and went on.

"Anyone who would like to join the drama club is invited to attend a planning meeting this afternoon at three o'clock in the auditorium.

Please come and join us for Bradley's hottest new club!"

I stepped away from the microphone, feeling a little better. If I got stage fright like this every time I got up to perform, I was going to have some awful career problems later on.

"That was great!" Katie told me later as we put away our books in our locker. "You sounded so calm."

"I sounded like a Munchkin," I groaned. "Did you hear that?"

"Only for a second," Katie consoled me. "I don't think anybody else even noticed."

"Definitely not," Randy said, coming up to us with Allison. "You had it nailed, Sabs. It's gonna go just great today."

I did feel relieved now that I realized the announcement had sounded okay. My friends are just the coolest — they always know how to calm me down.

"What about the ruby slippers?" I asked as we walked toward the auditorium. "Any ideas?"

My friends shook their heads. "Not yet," Katie said. "But don't worry. We'll think of something."

I stopped short in front of the auditorium. There wasn't a single person waiting at the door. The big, thick doors loomed above us.

"Hey, relax, Sabs," Katie advised me quietly. "It's not even five after three yet. There's plenty of time for kids to come. Let's give it a few minutes, okay?"

"Nobody's going to come!" I wailed. "I made a fool of myself this morning, and who's going to want to join a drama club whose president is a fool?"

"Why don't we go sit down, at least?" Allison suggested. "Didn't you say Mr. Metcalf was going to be here? Maybe he's waiting for us."

"Sure," Randy said, giving me a little push. "Let's go on in."

I pushed open the huge auditorium door, trying not to burst into tears over my big failure. As we walked inside, though, I had the biggest shock of my entire life. The whole auditorium was packed with kids waiting for us. They were all here for the drama club — every single one!

When they saw us come in, the kids started cheering and clapping. "Wow!" Randy whispered. "It's just like a rock concert!"

"Is that all for us?" I asked, looking around.

"It's all for you, Sabs." Allison smiled. "They're all waiting for you to get things going."

Ohmygosh! I suddenly realized just how much I'd taken on with this show. This wasn't going to some easy, last-minute thing. This was going to be three and a half weeks of really hard work.

The worst thing was, I didn't have the faintest idea what to do next. I knew I had to figure out how to get this club going. I just didn't know how I was going to get everything organized. What was my next step?

Luckily, Mr. Metcalf was already waiting at the piano. He had agreed to be our faculty adviser and to help with the music. He had the score from The Wizard of Oz and was playing bits of the songs. "Hi, team," he said cheerfully when I reached him. "How do you want to handle this?"

He was looking at me like he just knew I had a plan to deal with this whole mess and everything would go fine. I don't know exactly why, but whenever someone looks at me like that, I suddenly feel completely confident. That's just how I felt when I looked at Mr. Metcalf. I faced the kids all waiting for me.

"Hi, everybody!" I said loudly. "Welcome to the seventh-grade drama club!"

They all called back hellos to me, and I couldn't help smiling at Randy, Allison, and Katie. "I'll be the director for the Wizard of Oz and I'm really looking forward to a great show! The first thing we need to do is figure out who's going to be on which committee."

At that moment a familiar voice rang out from the back of the auditorium. "Why don't we have tryouts first?" called Stacy. "That's the way it's usually done."

"I agree with Sabrina," said Mr. Metcalf. "We need to find out who's interested in the different areas before we can have tryouts."

I looked at Mr. Metcalf gratefully and Stacy subsided in a huff.

"Okay," I said. "Would whoever would like to be in charge of the various committees, like props, costumes, lighting, and so on, please come up and say a few words. Then everyone will vote for the one they want to head each committee."

A few people came up to speak and then everybody voted. In the end, Allison became the stage manager, Katie was made publicity coordinator, and Randy was put in charge of costumes. Winslow Barton was the only one who volunteered to be in charge of lights and sound, and so he got that job. And my brother Sam was put in charge of building the sets. The only people who seemed to be unhappy about the choices were Stacy and her friends. But it wasn't my fault that my friends were chosen. It was a fair vote.

That all took less time than I had thought, so I decided to start auditions that same afternoon. There were a bunch of people there who wanted to be on the various committees and also be in the show.

"We're to do the auditions for the Scarecrow, the Tin Man, and the Cowardly Lion first. Who wants to play any of those parts?"

At least fifty hands went up. Mr. Metcalf invited those people down to the stage and had them stand in three lines — all the Scarecrows in one, Tin Men in another, and Lions in the third. Then he gave them the words for "If I Only Had a Brain" and I sat down right near the stage to listen.

Some of the singers were pretty good. A few

were really good. The rest were just awful. "Ow!" Randy whispered as she listened to one Scarecrow. "He sounds like he got caught in a washing machine!"

Behind us, Allison murmured, "Don't you want to take notes, Sabrina? So you can remember what you thought of each one?"

"Good idea!" I agreed. I had fixed up a special clipboard to use for the show, and it was full of blank notebook paper. Allison lent me a pen, and I started to write down short notes on each performer. It was tough, though. They got through the songs faster than I could write.

"Just give them numbers from one to ten," Katie suggested. "You know, if they're really good, they get a ten. If they're terrible, they get a one."

"Great idea, Katie," I said. "That way we can just pick from the nines and tens when we go to make final choices."

It seemed like the auditions for Dorothy's three friends and the Munchkins were going to last all afternoon. But finally the last singers were done, and I thanked everybody for coming and promised to pot a list after tomorrow's auditions for the people who made the show.

Then from somewhere far in the back of the auditorium I heard Stacy call out, "What about the auditions for Dorothy? Can't we do those today, too?"

"We'll audition for Dorothy and the rest of the parts tomorrow," I called. "Please come back then."

I saw Stacy stand up and stalk angrily toward the door. Then she turned back and said in a loud voice, "I must say, this is the most disorganized, most idiotic club I've ever had the misfortune to be a part of. I sure hope that I won't be embarrassing myself by being associated with it." And with that she stormed out of the auditorium, followed by Eva and Laurel. So much for my wish of no more trouble from Stacy!

Chapter Seven

That night after dinner Allison, Randy, Katie, and Winslow came over. We don't usually get together on school nights, but our parents agreed that since we were trying to set up this drama club, they could make one exception.

I already had pages of notes from the auditions and was looking them over. It was going to be easy to cut out some of the singers, but a lot of them were really good. I had eight people I really liked and we only had three roles to fill. The rest would be Munchkins. It was going to be tough. I was glad we'd decided that the heads of all the committees would decide on the casting.

I also had this megaphone which I found in our attic. Now I would really look, and sound, like a real director. Plus I wouldn't have to worry about straining my voice with shouting and all. I mean, Dorothy would have to have a good, strong voice. And I really, really wanted to play

Dorothy.

"Hi, Cinnamon," Katie greeted our dog as she came in. She patted Cinnamon's soft fur and sat down next to me. "You know, there's one part we haven't even thought about."

"What's that?" I asked. I was trying really hard to think of everything.

"Toto. Who's going to play Toto?" Katie asked.

I couldn't think of anything to say. I hadn't thought of that. It was going to be tough having a dog onstage, too. Big directors always say they don't want to work with dogs or babies. Thank goodness there were no babies in The Wizard of Oz. "Well, then," I said finally, "I guess we're going to need a dog."

"Did I hear you talking about Stacy?" Randy asked as she came in with Winslow.

"No, silly." Katie giggled. "We were trying to figure out who to use as Toto."

Randy bent down to pet my dog. "Well, what's wrong with Cinnamon? She's a dog, isn't she?"

"Sure she is!" I exclaimed. "And Cinnamon's great around people. She won't get upset or nervous. She'd be perfect."

Allison looked doubtfully at Cinnamon as she put her coat down. "I don't know, Sabs. She's awfully big for Toto, isn't she? I mean, Dorothy's supposed to pick up Toto in the play. Can you pick up Cinnamon?"

"No problemo," I said. "C'mere, Cinnamon." Cinnamon bounded over to me, and I bent down. Cinnamon doesn't mind being held, but she seemed to have gotten a lot heavier since the last time I picked her up. I was almost staggering once I got her off the ground. "Look at that," I gasped, trying to act very cool and relaxed. "Everything under control!"

Randy, Katie, and Allison tried to keep straight faces, but they just couldn't do it. In a minute they were all roaring with laughter. I tried to hold on to Cinnamon and stay serious, but it was impossible. I broke up, too, and the minute I did, Cinnamon jumped out of my arms, shook herself indignantly, and flounced off.

"Oh, Sabs, you looked so ridiculous!" Katie gasped. "You're so . . . and she's so . . ." She couldn't even finish. Allison was laughing so hard she couldn't talk, and Randy was wiping away tears. Winslow was trying to look serious, but I could tell that he was about to crack up.

"I don't think Cinnamon's going to cut it as Toto," Randy said finally. "We'll just have to use someone else's dog."

Just then my brothers Mark and Sam came down from their room looking for a snack.

"Are we having our casting meeting already?" Sam asked.

"Yes, we are," Katie told him.

"Right now we're looking for a Toto," Randy said. "Do you know anybody who has a dog that looks like Toto?"

"I know one," said Winslow. Then he got very busy playing with Cinnamon, who was now lying on the rug.

"Well, who is it, Winslow?" I demanded. "We have to get in touch with them right away."

"No — I don't think you really want to do that, Sabrina," Winslow said quickly. "In fact, why don't we just forget it?"

"Forget it? Why should we? Who is it, Winslow?" Katie asked.

I saw Mark's face light up, like he was suddenly on Winslow's wavelength. Then he also bent down to play with Cinnamon.

"Winslow's right, Sabs," he told me. "You

really don't want to know about it. Maybe you could borrow a stuffed dog, or something."

"No, a real dog is better," I insisted. "Come on, guys, if you know a dog we can use, tell us. This isn't fair."

"Well . . ." Winslow looked at Mark and Mark looked at Sam. I saw Sam's face light up just the way Mark's had. I faced him indignantly.

"Come on, Sam. Tell me!" I demanded.

"Well . . ." He looked over at his friends "Stacy just happens to have a real cute little dog, named Fluffy. He looks just like Toto."

Stacy! It figured.

"She'd never lend us her dog in a million years," Allison pointed out.

"She might," Sam said, looking hard at me.

It's a funny thing about being a twin. You look at each other sometimes, and you just know what the other one's thinking. In this case, I knew just what Sam was thinking.

"I will not!" I cried. "I will not let Stacy play Dorothy!"

Sam nodded. "I can understand that. But I'll bet you anything she won't lend you her dog unless she gets a part."

"At this point, I don't want her to be in the show at all!" I insisted. "Why should I spend three weeks in rehearsals with her if she's so determined to be difficult? I mean, she keeps saying how stupid the club is!"

"At least you'd get to boss her around," Winslow pointed out. "You're the director, Sabrina. She'd have to do just what you say."

I thought about that. It would be kind of neat to be telling Stacy what to do for a few weeks.

"Well, maybe," I agreed. "But not as Dorothy, and not if she doesn't join. I'll use a stuffed dog for Toto if I have to."

"Well, there is some good news," Sam told me. "Dad's agreed to donate all the material we need to build the sets. He'll give us wood, paint, nails — the works. He told me to figure out what we need, and said he'd bring it all home from the store over the weekend."

"Hey, that's great!" said Allison.

It really was. It was awesome of my father to give us all that stuff for our show. But I was still steaming about Stacy.

Katie sat down at the table. "What else do we need?" he asked.

"Well, besides Toto . . ." I looked at my list.

"There's a wand for Glinda, the presents the Wizard gives at the end, the bicycle for Miss Gulch..."

"And the ruby slippers," Randy reminded me. "Those are the most important."

"Where can we get those?" Katie pondered. "You think maybe one of the shoe stores in town would lend us a pair?"

"Only if we weren't actually going to wear them," Allison answered. "Once you wear a pair of shoes and the bottoms get scuffed, they can't sell them as new anymore."

"What about the original shoes from the movie?" I asked. I figured you might just as well think big. I'll bet the whole school would sit up and take notice if we could borrow Judy Garland's ruby slippers!

"Forget it, Sabs," Randy told me. "My father knows a guy who collects that kind of stuff. He said the ruby slippers are worth hundreds of thousands of dollars. Nobody would ever lend them to us, even if we could find them in time for the show."

"Maybe someone here in Acorn Falls owns red shoes that we could borrow," Allison suggested.

We all thought hard for a minute. Then Katie gave a little cry. Her face suddenly had the same expression on it that Nick's had when he thought of Stacy's dog, Fluffy.

"What is it, Katie?" I asked, fearing the worst.

"I just thought of the perfect shoes," Katie said unhappily. "They've got high heels and dark red sequins sewn all over them. They sort of sparkle when you hold them up to the light."

"But they sound great! Whose are they?" Allison asked.

Katie looked even unhappier. "Stacy's," she said. "She wore them on that TV show, 'Hitline U.S.A.'"

I couldn't think of a thing to say. Everybody at the table was quiet for a minute. It was bad enough that Stacy had the perfect dog for Toto. If she also had the perfect shoes for the ruby slippers, I might have to break down and consider having her in the show. It might be the only way to get the show on at all.

I looked down at the table and spotted the newspaper. I had forgotten to read my horoscope for the day, so I reached for it. Under Pisces, the horoscope read: "Look for ways to get the job done. It may mean asking for help in unusual places."

Boy, did that ever fit!

"What's it say, Sabs?" Randy asked.

I pushed the newspaper away. I wouldn't put Stacy in the play, and that was final. Not even my horoscope could make me! "Never mind. I won't do it, that's all. Nobody can make me put Stacy in the play!"

For the rest of the evening we discussed who to put in the parts we'd held auditions for that day and then everyone went home.

I didn't sleep well that night at all. I kept tossing and turning. When I finally fell asleep, I had the weirdest dream. I dreamt I was at the bottom of a well and couldn't get out.

Above me, outside the well, Stacy the Great and her clones were laughing at me, although I was terrified and knew I was going to break down and cry any minute.

Stacy told me the only way for me to get out was if she threw down her red shoes — the ones that looked just like Dorothy's ruby slippers. But she wouldn't throw them down unless I promised her a lot of things. She wanted me to turn over the office of class president to her. She wanted some of my favorite accessories, like my brown velvet hat and the gold combs for my hair. She even wanted me to give up my place among my friends, so she could be best friends with Katie, Randy, and Allison!

It was the worst nightmare I could remember! But it obviously had something to do with The Wizard of Oz. Everyone else seemed to think I'd never get the show off the ground if I couldn't borrow Stacy's stuff. I was beginning to think they were right, although I sure didn't want to admit it.

Then it came to me! I suddenly had the perfect idea of how to get Stacy's things and make everybody happy at the same time. It was going to be just great!

Chapter Eight

Thursday morning I was a little late getting started. Still, I'd already planned what I was going to wear — while tossing and turning in the middle of the night — so I actually managed to get to school on time.

"Hey, Sabs! What a great outfit!" said Katie. She was already at our locker, taking out books for first period.

I shoved my stuff inside and did a quick spin around, so she could see the rest.

"Do I look like a big-time director or what?" I asked.

"You look great," Allison assured me. She and Randy were waiting for us by our locker. They already had their books for first period.

"Very professional," Randy agreed. "You look a lot like the TV people my father works with. Very cool."

From Randy, that was a special compliment.

I thought I looked pretty good myself. I was wearing dull gold pants with a long-sleeved gold shirt and a deep red vest. My hair was pushed under the brown velvet tam Stacy the Great had wanted in my nightmare. I felt better having the hat close by. I figured Stacy wouldn't snatch it off my head in school!

"Listen, guys," I said, lowering my voice to a whisper, "I got a great idea last night."

"About the play?" Katie asked.

I nodded. "I'm going to get Stacy's stuff to use in the show and keep her happy without letting her play Dorothy."

"How?" Allison asked. "You know she'll want the best part for herself."

The bell rang before I could tell them anything else. We all split up, running for our classes. "I'll tell you at lunch," I yelled over my shoulder. "It's going to be a blast!"

Randy, Allison, and Katie had already started eating by the time I got to the lunchroom, but they'd saved me a place. They couldn't wait to hear my plan.

"Come on, Sabs, spill it!" Randy urged. "I can't wait to hear how we're going to outsmart Stacy the Great!"

I couldn't help enjoying the anticipation on the faces of my friends, so I waited until I'd swallowed my first bite of my tuna sandwich before I said, "I think we should let Stacy in the play after all."

"Let her in!" Randy shrieked. "You spent all of last night insisting you were going to keep her out!"

"What made you change your mind, Sabs?" Allison asked.

"Toto and the shoes," Katie guessed. "We really need them, don't we?"

"That's true," I agreed. "Besides, I think Stacy may have some real acting ability. We wouldn't want her to be deprived of an opportunity to show off her talent."

Randy's eyes gleamed. "I get the feeling that I'm going to like whatever you're thinking, Sabs."

"I'm glad," I told her, "because you and I have to work together. We really want the Wicked Witch of the West to look incredibly ugly, don't we?" I put a lot of emphasis on ugly.

Katie started to laugh. "Sabs, you are the best. You're going to give Stacy the part of the Wicked Witch, aren't you?"

"And make her wear green makeup on her face and a fake long nose —" Allison added, picking up my train of thought exactly.

"And warts," I interrupted her. "Lots and lots of warts. She'll need a lot of attention to costume and makeup, Randy. Think you can handle that?"

Randy grinned. "It'll be a pleasure. I'll take care of it personally."

"But there's one problem," said Katie. "Stacy will never agree to play the Witch."

"Oh yes she will," I said. Then I told them the plan we would put into action that very afternoon. I made sure they knew exactly how to behave and what to say.

"I don't know, Sabs," Katie protested. "I'm not sure I can say that about you. That's totally unfair!"

"Not to mention wrong," Randy chimed in.

"You have to say just what I tell you," I warned them. "Promise that you will?"

"Oh, I promise," Katie grumbled. "But I hate lying about my friends, even if they know about it in advance."

"Thanks." I grinned. "We know it's not true, but we've got to convince Stacy that it is!"

I couldn't help being pleased that my friends liked my idea. It really was the perfect answer. Suddenly none of us could wait for that afternoon's auditions!

I actually managed to get to the auditorium on time. There were a lot fewer people there today, since a bunch of people had already auditioned. I was a little worried, because I didn't see Stacy or the clones anywhere.

"There they are!" Randy whispered to me. "Way in the back. I guess Stacy still hates to admit she wants to be in the show."

I stood at the front of the auditorium with my clipboard and my megaphone. "Okay, everybody!" I called out. Boy, did my voice sound loud! "We'll start with the readings for the Wicked Witch. Will everyone who wants to play the Witch please come onstage?"

I'd really hoped that Stacy would get right up and head for the stage, but no such luck. She just sat there. Eva got up, though, along with about ten other girls. I gave them the scene to read where the Witch first appears.

Some of them sounded really good, and one girl did a perfect imitation of Margaret Hamilton, who played the Witch in the movie.

But I kept thinking of Toto and the ruby slippers and reminded myself not to forget Stacy.

When we finished with the Wicked Witch, I asked for the Glindas. There weren't as many, but I noticed Laurel came up. I was surprised, too: She was pretty good and very graceful. She might make a very good Glinda! Besides, the more of Stacy's friends I put in the play, the more she'd want to be in it.

Aunt Em was the next part, and I saw only a few girls. They were mostly taller and could look older, which would be perfect, since I'd look very young next to them, being so petite. I hate it when someone calls me short, but it's a fact that I'm just four feet ten and three-quarter inches right now!

Miss Gulch was the last role before Dorothy. In the movie, Margaret Hamilton played both parts. I guess maybe they didn't have a lot of money to spend on actresses. Here at Bradley, though, I thought it was a good idea to give someone else the part of Miss Gulch. It wasn't very big, but it would give another actress some time on the stage. There were only two girls trying out for the part, and I knew right away which one I wanted. The girl who did the

Margaret Hamilton imitation was back.

Finally we were up to Dorothy. Mr. Metcalf played the piano as almost every single girl tried out! Including me! I have to admit that my singing wasn't the best, but I knew I would make up for it with my acting skills. And besides, I still had three weeks to really learn the songs.

I was the last one to sing, and when I left the stage, Stacy was still sitting, stone-faced, in the auditorium. She had been one of the first to try out, but I guess she wanted to see the competition.

I picked up my megaphone and called out, "Thanks for coming, everybody. We'll post a cast list tomorrow morning next to Mr. Metcalf's office. See you at rehearsal!"

Then, just as I planned, I started walking off the stage and said loudly to my friends, "Let's go to Fitzie's for a soda, guys. I'm really thirsty."

I pretended to have just seen Stacy. "Oh, hi, Stacy! I didn't see you!" I said, trying to sound completely surprised.

Stacy tossed her blond hair over her shoulder, as though she hadn't even heard me. I started walking away, pretending to look at my clipboard.

"I've got to pick up some stuff. I'll meet you at Fitzie's!" I called to the others. As soon as I was outside, I raced for Fitzie's as fast as I could. If the plan worked, Allison, Randy, and Katie would bring Stacy there. I wanted to hear every single word!

I got to Fitzie's and found two vacant booths, back to back. I hid in one booth and tossed my notebook on the other to save it for my friends. Sure enough, a few minutes later, they walked in with Stacy. They were talking to her in low voices, as though they didn't want anybody else to hear. Everything looked perfect. I slid down in my booth to hear every word.

My friends sat in the vacant booth and ordered sodas. Stacy wasn't acting so haughty now. In fact, she sounded pretty miserable. Randy was acting really sympathetic toward her. "Look, Stacy," Randy said, "I know just how you feel. We're getting a little embarrassed by Sabrina, too."

"Embarrassed!" Stacy sniffed. "You know she's going to take the lead and all the credit for directing — and all you feel is embarrassed?"

"But that's the point," Katie chimed in. "We don't think she should be doing all that herself."

"Thank goodness we talked her out of the

really good part," Allison added. She sounded relieved. I never knew Allison was such a good actress.

Stacy's voice came back suspiciously. "What do you mean? What really good part?"

"At first she was going to play the Wicked Witch," Randy explained. "But we finally talked her out of that one!"

"It would be better for the play," Stacy said snidely. "She might even be able to do it without makeup."

I almost jumped out of my booth when I heard that. Talk about insulting! I wasn't sure I'd be able to control myself much longer. But I reminded myself that I was an actress, and self-control was part of my job. So I managed to keep from bursting right into the conversation, and listened as Katie took over.

"Imagine Sabrina playing the toughest part in the show and directing, too," Katie said to Stacy. "It would be impossible."

"Anyway, it takes a really great actress to play the Wicked Witch," Randy jumped in. "Frankly, between you and me, I don't think Sabrina's that good."

Stacy was very quiet. She appeared to be

thinking it over. Finally she said, "She hasn't made up her mind about who to cast as the Witch yet, has she?"

"Well, no," Allison answered. "There were some pretty good actresses up there today."

"I think we need someone better," Randy said in a confiding way. "You know, somebody who can really stand out. Somebody who can really take over the stage."

There was another pause. Then Stacy said, "I was thinking about trying out for it."

"Hey, you'd be great!" Randy said immediately. "How come you didn't read for it?"

"You know Sabrina would never give me the part," said Stacy. "She's always been jealous of me."

I gnashed my teeth in the second booth. Jealous of Stacy the Great? Give me a break!

"You're absolutely right," Katie said thoughtfully. "Why should you get the best part and maybe even steal the show right out from under her nose?"

"I'd be great in that part!" Stacy burst out. I knew we were just about home free. Now she wanted to play the Witch!

"You really would be great," Allison said, a

little sadly. She appeared to be thinking hard. I couldn't believe Allison never wanted to be in the school plays. She was a natural. Then she seemed to brighten. "Hey, wait a minute! I've got a great idea!"

"What is it?" Randy asked.

"Look, Randy, you know we're in a bind. We need a dog to play Toto and a pair of red shoes for the ruby slippers."

"I've got a dog!" Stacy said quickly. "Fluffy looks just like Toto. And I have a great pair of red shoes, too!"

"Really?" Katie said in her most innocent tone. "Isn't that amazing!"

"Wait. Here's the idea," Allison said. "If you lend us your dog and your shoes for the play, I'll bet Sabrina would have to give you the part! She wouldn't have any choice!"

"Yeah, she'd really be stuck," Stacy said thoughtfully. She took a sip of her soda. "Hey, I think that's a great idea. I'll give her a call and offer her my dog and the red shoes, but only if she gives me the part of the Wicked Witch."

"She can't possibly refuse," Allison assured her. "You've really got her in a corner."

"Thanks a lot, guys," Stacy said in her nicest

voice. "I'm really glad I'm going to get in the play after all."

"Anytime, Stacy," Randy said. "You're really getting us out of trouble. We owe you one!"

Stacy got up and marched toward the door. She turned around and sang out to my friends, "See you at rehearsals!"

"Remember," Randy called, "don't tell Sabrina we told you. Top secret!"

"Top secret!" Stacy agreed. She hurried out.

We waited about five minutes, until we were all sure that Stacy wouldn't be back. Then Randy tapped on the top of the booth. "Mission accomplished, Sabs!" she said, laughing.

We all burst into laughter. We were getting Stacy's dog, the ruby slippers, and Stacy — in the worst getup we could devise! And I could play Dorothy, just like I'd always wanted to!

It was just too good not to celebrate. So I had a double chocolate-chip sundae with everything. After all, sometimes you have to go right over the top!

Chapter Nine

We started rehearsals on Monday. During that first week I was a little surprised at how much work I had to do. Despite my singing in the audition, the casting committee decided to let me play Dorothy. They knew I was dying to play Dorothy, and agreed that I deserved something for all the work I was doing! So I had to learn my lines in the script and all the songs, which I knew anyway.

Then I also had to worry about all the other things I'd always taken for granted. Every single person connected with the show wanted to talk to me about something. It made me feel really important, but I also began to think there weren't enough hours in the day. Randy always wanted to talk to me about costumes and make-up. Allison and Katie were working up terrific posters to advertise the show. Winslow usually managed to corner me at least once a day to ask about the sound and tech booth in the auditorium. Sam wanted to talk about how to fix up our sets.

Stacy had brought her little dog, Fluffy, and her red shoes to the first rehearsal. Since Dorothy had to wear the ruby slippers for most of the show, I immediately slipped backstage to try them on.

They really were beautiful shoes. They glittered just like the ones Judy Garland had worn in the movie, and they had real high heels, too. My mother won't let me wear heels yet, but she couldn't really object if they were part of my costume for the play.

I slipped them on and stood in front of a dusty mirror. They were perfect! Now I really felt like Dorothy!

"Sabrina," Mr. Metcalf was calling. "We need you onstage."

Quickly I hurried onto the stage. There were a mass of people standing around, all looking confused.

When I reached the stage, Mr. Metcalf whispered, "They're waiting for you to tell them what to do. You're the director."

I'd been so busy preparing as an actress that I

hadn't thought about what I'd have to do with the other people in the cast. But no one was going to do anything unless I told them what I wanted them to do.

Finally I figured I'd better get started with something, or we'd waste the whole afternoon. I grabbed my megaphone and told all the people playing Munchkins to come to the edge of the stage. I was going to teach them the dance for "Ding! Dong! The Witch Is Dead!"

I'd worked out a great dance routine in front of my mirror at home. It was very simple, but I figured that with the Munchkin costumes and makeup, they'd look really lively doing it.

I stood in front of everyone and asked Mr. Metcalf to play the song. Then I started the dance. But I'd forgotten I was still wearing Stacy's shoes, and unfortunately, she has much bigger feet than I do. When I was standing in front of the mirror backstage, it hadn't occurred to me to check the size. They just looked so good on my feet.

Now, though, I was skipping and dancing — or trying to. The instant I kicked my right foot into the air, the shoe came flying off my foot and hit Katie!

Everyone roared with laughter. It was so embarrassing!

"I'm sorry, Katie," I called. "Did I hurt you?"

Katie rubbed her arm. "I don't think so, Sabs." She handed back the shoe and whispered to me, "Better stuff some paper inside. At least that'll help them stay on."

"Good idea," I agreed. I felt really stupid calling a break to stuff paper in the shoes, but I didn't have any choice. The notebook paper was stiff against my toes, but at least the shoes stayed on this time.

I started the dance again, and this time everyone joined in. It was an easy dance to learn, so in a few minutes almost everyone got it right. I wanted them to sing and dance the whole song together, to see how it looked, but before I could ask Mr. Metcalf to play it again and explain to the cast what I wanted to do, Randy pulled me aside.

"Sabs, we got problems," she announced breathlessly. "We need you backstage right now."

"What is it?" I asked. I didn't want to leave the rehearsal, but Randy sounded urgent.

"You'd better hurry," Winslow said gloomily.

I had no choice. I called another break. Mr. Metcalf came over to me. "Maybe I should rehearse the songs with them while you're gone," he suggested.

I knew he was concerned about wasting time, but I also knew that I was the director. I had to be there for every single minute of rehearsals, so I could keep track of what was going on. If I missed his singing rehearsal, I might get behind. Then I'd never catch up, and the whole show could go to pieces. I couldn't let that happen!

"No, it's okay, Mr. Metcalf," I told him. "I'll be back in just a second."

Then I followed Winslow and Randy backstage to the tech board. We all stared down at the mass of wires jutting out of the board.

"What's that?" I asked.

"That's our sound board," Winslow said unhappily. "Somebody must have disconnected it after the last show and never put it back together."

"Don't you know how?" I asked. Winslow was so smart, I figured he could do just about anything.

But he shook his head. "I've never done

sound for a show before. I don't have any idea what to hook up where."

"Well, maybe we can do the show without it," I said, hoping they'd both agree with me. "Would that be a problem?"

"Only if you want people to hear what you're saying," Randy answered.

"You'd better talk to Mr. Hansen about getting somebody to hook up the sound again," Winslow advised me. "It probably won't take more than a couple of hours."

I made a note on my clipboard. That was the first of many. It seemed as though every day I made more and more notes on the clipboard. Unfortunately, I wrote down more things to do than I actually got done!

I went back to the rehearsal. The Scarecrow, Tin Man, and Lion were ready to learn their dance for "We're Off to See the Wizard." As Dorothy, I was supposed to dance on the Yellow Brick Road with them. So I had to teach them the steps and get in line with them so we could do the whole routine together.

Unfortunately, I hadn't thought about the boys playing the parts. Arizonna, who was playing the Tin Man, was a laid-back surfer type from California. When I asked him to show a little more enthusiasm, he just shrugged. His idea of dancing was sort of shuffling down the Yellow Brick Road.

At the same time, Rich Carlyle, who played the Scarecrow, was a lot like Ray Bolger, who played the Scarecrow in the movie. Rich was a basketball player on Bradley's varsity team, and he bounced when he walked. He was also one of the cutest boys in the whole seventh grade. I figured since Dorothy spent a lot of time with the Scarecrow, I'd have plenty of time to get to know Rich really well. I already knew I liked his singing voice and his big blue eyes a whole lot!

Billy Dixon was playing the Lion. Billy was tall enough for the Lion, but he was no more a coward than I was a little girl from Kansas. In fact, he was once a real troublemaker at Bradley. He sort of swaggered through his dance steps. So between Rich's bouncing, Arizonna's shuffling, and Billy's swaggering, we looked pretty weird. I kept saying that we had to dance down the Yellow Brick Road together, but they didn't seem to get it. It was very discouraging.

When I gave them a break, Mr. Metcalf asked me to sing "Over the Rainbow" with the piano.

Singing is not really my specialty, but actresses have to learn to do all kinds of things. So it didn't really bother me that I didn't sing like Judy Garland. As long as I could remember the words and sing on key, I'd be okay. I knew it was my acting the part of Dorothy that would bring the house down.

When I opened my mouth, though, the sound that came out was high and squeaky. I couldn't believe it! Mr. Metcalf didn't seem upset at all. He just went back and played the introduction again. I opened my mouth again and somehow got out the firrst few notes."

Ohmygosh! I sounded worse than before! I sounded like Minnie Mouse on helium! I could feel the tears welling up in my eyes.

To make things worse, Arizonna, Rich, and Billy were sitting in the audience. Rich probably didn't mean to, but he started to laugh. Once he got going, everybody else joined in. Even Mr. Metcalf turned his head away from me so I couldn't see him grinning.

I felt horrible. As soon as I could take a deep breath, I grabbed my megaphone and told everybody that rehearsal was over. We'd start work on the farm scenes tomorrow. There wouldn't be any singing, just acting. I figured I could handle that easier than singing and dancing rehearsals.

Somehow holding that megaphone really helped. It made me feel in control. The second I put it down, I wanted to run away and hide. But once I stepped offstage, about a thousand people were crowding around wanting to talk to me.

"Hey, Sabs, what do you want to do about the Witch's castle?" Sam asked me, holding up a length of chicken wire.

"Don't forget to talk to Mr. Hansen about the sound board," Winslow added, getting ready to leave.

"When is the band coming in to rehearse?" Randy asked. "We'll need to hear how everybody sounds with the band."

"Sabs, are you okay?" Katie asked. She could see how upset I was, and she waved everyone else away so we could be alone. "You look a little frazzled."

"I'm fine," I managed to say.

Allison and Randy crowded around me. "You're trying to do an awful lot here. Maybe it's a little too much for one person to handle," Allison suggested softly.

"Yeah. You've got so much to do as the director, it's going to be tough playing Dorothy, too," Randy chimed in.

I knew that they all cared about me, but I couldn't even think about giving up the part of Dorothy. It was the perfect part for me and I knew it. Nobody else could play it the way I could! Besides, since I was doing so much work, it was only fair that I get a chance to do something I really wanted to do.

"I can handle it," I insisted. "Everything's going to work out just great."

Just then Mr. Metcalf came over. My friends cleared a space for him, and he smiled at me. I tried to blink away the tears in my eyes, so he'd think I was right on top of things. "Maybe you should post notices for the band to come in," he suggested. "We should start them working with you during the rehearsals."

"That's a great idea, Mr. Metcalf," I answered. I couldn't believe how calm I sounded. Obviously he thought so, too, because he smiled at me again.

"This is a big chunk to bite off, Sabrina," he pointed out. "You've got so much to think about with your directing . . ."

I had a terrible feeling I knew what he was going to say. "Yes?" I asked.

"Well" — he glanced at the other girls and turned back to me — "maybe you'll do some thinking about the part of Dorothy. It's a big responsibility playing Dorothy even if you weren't directing. With the directing, too, I'm afraid you'll burn yourself out."

Now Mr. Metcalf was trying to talk me out of the part!

"Oh, no, Mr. Metcalf," I assured him. "I've got it together. My voice just didn't sound very good this afternoon because I was talking to the other actors first. I think maybe I strained it a little. Let's change things around. I'll do all my singing before I start directing the others. That way my voice will be fresh."

He hesitated. "That's a good idea, Sabrina," he said finally. "Why don't we try it that way tomorrow?"

My friends and I left school together and walked slowly for a few blocks. Nobody said anything. Then Katie said suddenly, "That was a great idea, Sabs! All you really need to pull this thing off is a little organization."

"Sure," Allison agreed. "If you budget your

time properly, you can probably handle the whole thing."

"Exactly," I agreed. It was a relief to see my friends backing me up once more.

"Maybe we should have production meetings every day at lunch," Randy remarked. "Then we won't be bothering you during rehearsals and you can do your acting and directing in peace. We'll wait until lunch the next day to tell you what needs to be done backstage."

"That's a great idea, Randy!" I cried. "I'm sure that'll make all the difference!"

I felt a lot better as I said good-bye to my friends and turned toward home. I could already see things shaping up!

Chapter Ten

Every day during those first two weeks, I had school all day and rehearsal right afterward. Then I rushed home to do my homework and fell into bed, so tired I could hardly think. I never even got the chance to read my horoscopes anymore, and I couldn't remember the last time I'd seen an issue of Young Chic.

On the following Tuesday night I had to write an English paper for Ms. Staats. By the time I got to bed, it was almost midnight. Naturally, I had a lot of trouble getting up Wednesday morning and I just got to school in time for the first bell.

I had trouble listening in English. My eyes felt all gritty from staying up so late the night before. Maybe if I closed them for a second, they'd feel a little better.

Slam! Something crashed in the front of the room, and my head snapped right up. "Sabrina, I'm so sorry to wake you," Ms. Staats said sharply.

Oh, no! I hadn't realized I was actually dozing in class! I could hear giggles all around me, especially from the corner where Stacy the Great sat with Laurel and Eva.

"I'm sorry, Ms. Staats," I said quickly. "I was up very late last night."

I could see Randy, Allison, and Katie looking at me sympathetically. They knew I wasn't goofing off. It was working so hard that kept me up late.

Still, the show was really shaping up. Keeping the rehearsals separate from the technical problems had really helped a lot. The actors started to do a lot better with their parts, even though I still hadn't memorized all my lines yet. I told myself it wasn't a big deal, I'd seen the movie a hundred times, and I'd find time to learn the lines very soon. It just seemed like there just was never enough time.

It was all worth it, though, I told myself. This was the big time. Sometimes you had to make personal sacrifices to achieve great things in your career.

The truth was, I was getting pretty proud of the show. Everybody was terrific in their parts, even Stacy's little dog, Fluffy. Fluffy never moved unless I told him to, and the minute I picked him up, he would lick my hand, just as if I was really Dorothy and he was really my pet!

Stacy was even getting into it. She had a really neat cackle that she used as the Witch, and she was very nice about my suggestions. If I asked her to move a certain way on the stage, she obeyed immediately. It was actually kind of fun to be ordering her around a little!

Randy and the costume crew had done a really super job on all the costumes and make-up. But she really outdid herself on Stacy's witch outfit. We stopped rehearsal early one afternoon so she could show the actors what they'd be wearing.

"And here's yours, Stacy," Randy said sweetly, opening a box. "Won't you look authentic!"

Stacy took one look at the costume she was holding up and gave this sort of whimper. Randy had designed a piece of black oilcloth with a hole at the top for the head and holes for the arms to go through. It was so long it swept the floor, and there was a piece of the ugliest rope imaginable to tie it at the waist. Then Randy had dirtied up the oilcloth with chalk and dust, so it looked like the Witch had worn it for years and never washed it. It was really disgusting. She'd even found a stringy black wig for Stacy to wear. The whole horrible thing was capped off with a huge black hat that had to be at least three feet high.

"And wait until you see the makeup," Randy went on. "I got the coolest shade of green paint for your face. Unless you want to wear gold instead?"

Stacy was so shocked she couldn't open her mouth. Randy pretended not to notice. She went on, "Great. We'll use the green. We'll black out a couple of your teeth in front, too. You'll look so evil, Stacy! It's going to be great!"

Then Randy handed me my costume. She'd copied it almost exactly from Judy Garland's dress in the movie. It was a very simple checked skirt with a white blouse over it, and two suspenders that looped over the skirt and blouse and fastened at my waist. It was a little big, but Randy told me we could pin it up tonight and sew it up later, in time for the show. We'd already put pads in the ruby slippers, so I didn't fall out of them every time I walked across the stage. In fact, I was rehearsing in them, so I'd be comfortable when I wore them during the show.

I watched everybody else take their costumes from Randy. Laurel was thrilled with her Glinda costume. It was big, white, and puffy, with a beautiful gauze skirt. She walked over to Stacy with it.

"Isn't this great?" she said.

"Oh, shut up!" Stacy snapped. The last thing Stacy needed was to see a beautiful dress on someone else, when she knew how terrible she was going to look!

A moment later, Mr. Metcalf called me over. He was talking to Mr. Hansen, who was nodding and smiling. "Well, Sabrina," Mr. Metcalf said, "looks like we've got some big news for you!"

"Hello, Sabrina," Mr. Hansen said heartily, with his usual phony smile. "I told Mr. Metcalf we wanted a big favor, but he told me to talk to the director!"

I smiled at Mr. Metcalf. He must think I'm doing a pretty good job if he wanted the principal to speak to me personally about his big favor. "Yes, Mr. Hansen," I said, feeling very confident. "What can I do for you?"

"Well, Sabrina," Mr. Hansen answered, "the

teachers and I are getting very curious about your show. The students and Mr. Metcalf have said it's just wonderful. You see, some of the faculty won't be able to attend the opening night, and they're a little disappointed. I wonder whether you'd do a little informal performance for us. It wouldn't have to be as elaborate as the real thing, of course, but it's a chance for you to have an audience for your dress rehearsal, and we might have some pointers for you afterward. What do you say?"

Wow! A special dress rehearsal for the teachers and the principal of Bradley? That would be a real kick! I just stood there with my mouth open, not sure what to say.

Mr. Metcalf saw my confusion and jumped in. "I told him the decision was all yours, Sabrina," he told me. "In fact, I've been telling him how just how much responsibility you've taken for this show. She's done it all," he told Mr. Hansen. "Lights, costumes, music — she's been involved in every phase of this show from start to finish. It's a real achievement, especially since she's acting in it, too!"

"That's quite a stunt!" Mr. Hansen boomed. "Not many seventh graders are that versatile,

Sabrina. We'll be looking forward to seeing the results. So how about that dress rehearsal? When would you like to do it?"

I thought quickly. Opening night was a week from Friday, which gave us another ten days to rehearse. Maybe it would be better to give the show earlier, so we could use the teachers' comments to make our final adjustments. Of course, I hadn't gotten my own part completely memorized yet, but I decided I'd just stay up late tonight and learn the whole thing by heart. I was getting used to some pretty long hours with this show, anyway.

"How about this Friday?" I said finally. "Then you can tell us how you like it, and if there are problems, we'll still have time to fix them before opening night."

"Excellent idea, Sabrina!" Mr. Hansen approved. "I'll tell the faculty to be ready for a special dress rehearsal of The Wizard of Oz this Friday night, and we can meet afterward so they can talk to you about it."

Boy, that sounded pretty awesome! Imagine hobnobbing with the teachers after our show so they could give us their suggestions! It sounded like when my favorite actors and actresses met the Queen of England, or something.

When the rehearsal was over, I told everybody about the special performance for the teachers. Arizonna and Billy Dixon were especially thrilled. They'd gotten their skipping coordinated down the Yellow Brick Road, and they were really good singers, too. Rich Carlyle bounced around even more than usual. He loved his Scarecrow costume and couldn't wait to act in front of the faculty. Randy and Winslow were excited, too. They'd get a chance to see how the lights and sound worked during a real performance.

Only Stacy was quiet. She kept looking at her ugly witch's outfit, then staring at the floor. I was actually beginning to feel a little sorry for her. After all, I was using her dog and her shoes to play Dorothy, the best part in the show. And here she was, playing the Witch and looking really horrible in front of all the teachers and her father and all the kids in school.

I couldn't stop thinking about the early performance. Katie, Randy, and Allison came over to my house for a little while after rehearsal. We all needed to relax a little. Katie was fixing up a tray with healthy snacks like popcorn and sparkling water. I was glad she knew my house so well. At that point, I was so tired, I didn't think I could stand up long enough to put everything together on the tray.

It seemed like I got more exhausted every day. My clipboard was always full of notes and things to do, and I spent a lot of my free periods during the day dealing with ticket sales and publicity. All the actors were supposed to take packets of tickets to sell, as soon as we got the tickets from the school printer.

"They're finally here!" Katie announced when she set down the tray. "I haven't even opened them yet, Sabs. I thought you should see them first."

I hardly even remembered ordering the tickets. Allison had offered to do it for me, but I insisted that it was the director's job to supervise everything in the show. So I wrote down what we wanted the tickets to say and took it to the printer right before class one morning. I remember I was very tired, especially since I'd been up really late studying for a math test the night before, and the printer had asked me nicely if I was sure I wanted them to say exactly what I'd written. I said I did.

Now I watched as Katie slit open the box and pulled out the tickets. "Oh, no!" she gasped. "They're awful!"

"What's wrong?" I asked, getting up to look over her shoulder. She was right. They were awful. The title of the show was printed "THE WAZIRD OF OZ"! I couldn't believe it! Suddenly I remembered the printer asking me about the order. Was I really so tired, I'd written it down that way for him to copy?

"Oh, no!" Randy groaned. "Look at the next line. Even the dates are wrong!"

We all looked below the title of the show. Instead of listing performances on the sixteenth, seventeenth, and eighteenth, the tickets read the fourteenth, fifteenth, and sixteenth!

"We'll never get them printed again before the show," Allison said. "Can we fix these?"

Katie looked grimly at the whole miserable mess. "I guess we'll have to cross out the title and the dates and write them in by hand with a black marker."

"You mean every ticket?" I asked, shocked. "That would take forever!"

"How else can we use these things?" Randy asked. "And we'll have to do them tonight, if

you want to start selling them at school tomorrow."

"But we have to do the posters tonight!" I
wailed. "We can't do both!"

"It's okay, Sabs," Katie said quickly. "How
about if we let the rest of the promotion committee do the posters over the weekend? They don't
really need to go up before Monday, anyway.
And then we can do the tickets tonight."

"And maybe Mr. Hansen will let you go on
the P.A. again to advertise the dates," Allison
put in. "That way everyone in school will know
the right dates and times and everything."

Suddenly I felt a whole lot better. "Thanks,
guys," I told them gratefully. "I guess that's
what we'll have to do."

So we all sat there and attacked the tickets.
Even though I was really worn out, it felt good
to be with my friends. I couldn't believe how far
we'd come. Here I was, about to star in a show I
directed myself! And in front of the whole faculty, too!

Chapter Eleven

Friday night's dress rehearsal was a really big deal. Even though Mr. Hansen had said the teachers didn't expect a full-blown performance, I wanted everything to be perfect. I got permission to skip my morning classes to help set the lights in the auditorium and run a sound check. I also watched the band set up and rehearse and even supervised Randy while she and her crew did all the makeup.

I'd had so much to do, in fact, that I still hadn't memorized all my lines. I wasn't too worried, though. I knew the songs cold, even if I still squeaked a little during "Over the Rainbow." The rest of the cast knew all their lines, and the songs and the dances really looked great. I really felt like the whole show had come together. Nothing could stop us now!

Katie helped me dress in my Dorothy costume and braid my hair into pigtails. Randy didn't have to make me up, since I was just using regular stage makeup to emphasize my eyes and mouth. Everyone else had to be very made-up so that they would look weird, but Dorothy's just supposed to look like a girl. I figured I qualified for that.

"You look perfect, Sabs!" Katie exclaimed when I finished. "Just like Judy Garland!"

"If only I could sing like her, too," I cracked. But I was too happy to be nervous. We were laughing when Allison knocked on the door of the rehearsal room.

"You ready, Sabs?" she asked.

I took a deep breath. I could feel the butterflies swimming around in my stomach. "I'm ready," I called.

"Okay. We're starting. Get on stage," Allison called back. When I opened the door, she grinned at me. "Break a leg out there."

I gave her a thumbs-up sign and hurried to the stage. The actors playing Uncle Henry and Aunt Em were already there, waiting for me. In a minute, we heard the band start the theme music. This was it!

The first scene went fine. Everyone knew what they were supposed to do, and they did it just right. Winslow and Randy had hooked up this neat slow-motion slide showing the cyclone, which they flashed on a screen in front of the stage. When the screen went up, we were supposed to be in Munchkinland.

I had Stacy's dog, Fluffy, in my arms as I walked around Munchkinland. I hadn't really seen the set, because I was too busy running around with other errands while they were painting it. So when I looked at it, I really was looking at it for the first time.

Suddenly Laurel, playing Glinda, appeared on my left. I thought she was supposed to be on my right, and I was so startled I stepped back, into exactly the wrong place. There was a little bush behind me, with Munchkins hiding behind it. I hit the bush and went right over, dropping Fluffy and landing on the Munchkins!

I don't think I've ever been so embarrassed in my whole life. The audience started to laugh.

Quickly I picked myself up. Glinda said, "Are you a good witch or a bad witch?"

I opened my mouth to answer, and realized I couldn't think of the next line. In fact, I couldn't think of any of my lines! It was like falling into the bush had made me forget everything in the script all at once.

I knew I should make something up, but I couldn't think of anything at all. I stood looking at Glinda with my mouth open, and Laurel, in her white gown with her wand, was frozen, too. Finally she repeated her question.

Allison, in the wings, was whispering to me frantically. She was really hard to hear. It sounded like, "Aba-daba-call. Oh, hail, Kansas."

I knew that wasn't exactly right, but that's just what I said. "Aba-daba-call. Oh, hail, Kansas."

Now the audience was really laughing. I thought I was going to die right there onstage. My mind was a complete blank. It was a little like studying too hard for a test. When the brain finally snaps, everything goes with it. I couldn't remember the movie, I couldn't remember my lines . . . to tell the truth, I wasn't even really sure who I was either!

Finally Laurel took charge of the scene. She said quickly, "Oh, I guess you aren't a witch at all. What's your name?"

I managed, "I'm Dorothy." But I knew that wasn't the whole line.

Still, Laurel picked it up and went on from

there. "You said you were from Kansas? Well, you aren't in Kansas now. You're . . ." She was having trouble, too, because her dialogue depended on mine, and she was trying to do both at once. I looked frantically into the wings and saw Allison trying to give me my lines. I saw her lips moving and realized she wanted me to say, "I'm Dorothy Gale. From Kansas."

I remembered now. I turned around and said loudly, "I'm Dorothy Gale. From Kansas."

But while I'd been looking at Allison, Laurel had started singing to the Munchkins, and they were already starting to sing, too. So I was speaking my line five minutes too late, and right in the middle of a song! It was getting worse and worse.

Stacy appeared on cue. She and Laurel managed to cover most of my dialogue so all I had to do was nod. For a minute I thought we might be able to pull it off after all. Then I had to grab the ruby slippers and put them on.

By the time I did that, I was so nervous and upset, I dug my fingers right into the bottom of the shoes. The pads we'd put in flew right out. As I looked at the audience, I saw one of them actually hit Mr. Hansen! I wanted to lie down right on the stage and die. I didn't think I could live through this show. It was a nightmare.

I was almost in tears by the time I got the shoes on. Allison saw me in the wings, ready to fall apart. "Don't think about it, Sabs!" she whispered. "Just get back out there!"

"I can't," I moaned. "Everything's ruined."

"Get going!" she said sternly. "You've got a lot of people depending on you. You can't let them down!"

She pushed me back out, but by then I couldn't really walk. The shoes were just too big for me without the pads, and I couldn't scrunch my feet into them so they'd stay on. I finally ended up shuffling across the stage. It was the only way to keep my feet and the shoes together.

The minute I had to dance on the Yellow Brick Road, though, it was all over. There was no way to keep those shoes on. I decided quickly that I'd better dance without them. So I took them off, put them in my little basket, waved goodbye to the Munchkins, and danced off in my ankle socks.

It probably looked very weird, because I heard a lot of strangled giggles, both in the audience and on the stage. But at that moment I just didn't care.

By the time the show was over, I was a wreck. Everything was ruined. The teachers applauded a lot when we took our bows, but I had trouble keeping myself from crying right there onstage. This was the worst night of my entire life. I hadn't remembered a single line since Munchkinland, and even though Allison kept calling the lines to me, I couldn't hear her over the music and the other actors.

Nobody said anything to me as we came off-stage and started getting ready for the reception. Katie smiled at me sympathetically, but I just couldn't talk to her. If I did, I knew I'd end up crying and really making a fool of myself. I'd have to quit the show. I didn't know what else to do to fix the mess I'd made.

When Mr. Hansen came up to me and said, "Ah, Dorothy herself. Quite a job, Sabrina," that was the end. I started to cry right there, in front of everybody. I ran off to the rehearsal rooms. I didn't care if I got expelled from school for being rude to the principal. I just wanted to get away where no one would find me and tell me how I'd ruined my own show. You might say I wanted to go over the rainbow myself!

Chapter Twelve

Sabrina calls Katie.

EMILY: Hello, Campbell-Beauvais resi-
              dence.

SABRINA: Emily? This is Sabrina. Can I talk
              to Katie, please? It's very impor-
              tant.

EMILY: Hold on, Sabrina. Katie's just com-
              ing in. . . . Katie! Telephone!

Katie picks up the phone.

KATIE: Hello?

SABRINA: Katie, it's Sabs.

KATIE: Sabs! Are you all right? I've been
              so worried!

SABRINA: Oh, Katie, last night was the worst
              night of my whole life. Everybody
              must think I'm a real crackpot!

KATIE: No they don't. Everybody knows
              how hard you've worked. You just

got a little overwhelmed, that's all.

SABRINA: Thanks, Katie. That helps. But what can I do? I never had time to memorize all my lines, and when I fell over that bush, every line I did know went right out of my head.

KATIE: Look, Sabs, it'll be okay. You've got a whole week to make changes.

SABRINA: That's true.

KATIE: Maybe you should call Randy and Allison, too. Maybe they'll have some ideas.

SABRINA: That's a good idea. I'll call them now.

KATIE: Let me know what happens.

SABRINA: I will. Thanks, Katie! Good-bye!

KATIE: Take it easy, Sabs.

Sabrina calls Randy.

RANDY: Ola?

SABRINA: Randy? It's Sabs.

RANDY: Sabs! How are you feeling? Better?

SABRINA: Well, at first I definitely wanted to leave Acorn Falls forever, but Katie talked me out of it.

RANDY: Good. 'Cause I was watching

things from the lighting booth, and you don't have a thing to worry about.

SABRINA: Randy, how can you say that? The whole show was a mess from beginning to end!

RANDY: Not the whole show, Sabs. Everything went fine, except that you've been trying to do way too much. You can't play the lead in a show and direct it and supervise everybody, too. Nobody can do that much!

SABRINA: But, Randy, I don't want to give up being in the show!

RANDY: Look, Sabs. You've only got one week left. You have to make some changes. If you don't, today might be a picnic compared to opening night!

SABRINA: I couldn't stand that!

RANDY: Well, most of the show is in great shape. You've got great sets, great actors, the band's good, the lights are awesome. But you've got to cut down on your own workload.

	My dad would never take on what you took on, and he directs for a living. Why don't you think about cutting back a little?
SABRINA:	Well, maybe you're right, Randy.
RANDY:	I know you can pull it off. You've got to delegate some authority now, or the whole thing'll fall apart. You can do it. You're the most together director I know.
SABRINA:	Thanks, Randy. Right now I don't feel too together, but I guess you're right. I'll call Allison and ask her about it.
RANDY:	Good idea, Sabs. Al always has great ideas.
SABRINA:	That's true. Bye, Ran.
RANDY:	Ciao.

Sabrina calls Allison.

CHARLIE:	This-is-Charlie-who-are-you?
ALLISON:	Charlie! Give me the phone! Hello, this is Allison Cloud.
SABRINA:	Allison, it's Sabs.
ALLISON:	Sabrina! We've been so worried about you!

101

SABRINA: I know. I've been talking to Katie and Randy.

ALLISON: How do you feel?

SABRINA: I'd been thinking about maybe running away to a desert island somewhere, but I guess that isn't really practical.

ALLISON: Definitely not. Suppose Stacy's on the next island? (Sabrina giggles.)

SABRINA: Thanks, I needed that. Randy says I'll have to delegate authority if the show's going to work.

ALLISON: What do you think?

SABRINA: I hate to admit it, but I guess she's right.

ALLISON: So what are you going to delegate?

SABRINA: Well . . . I guess you and Katie can handle the tickets and publicity without my help.

ALLISON: Great. That'll make your life a lot easier. And what about the acting?

SABRINA: What do you mean?

ALLISON: Sabs, the reason you got so mixed up today was that you didn't have enough time to memorize your lines. Don't you think that —

SABRINA: Oh, no, Al! I can't give up acting in the show! That's my favorite part of all this!

(Allison thinks for a moment.)

ALLISON: Well, look. Dorothy's a huge part. You don't even have enough time to learn it thoroughly before next Friday.

SABRINA: What are you thinking, Al?

ALLISON: Well . . . how about taking another part instead?

(Sabrina is quiet for a moment.)

SABRINA: Which part, Al?

ALLISON: Well . . . how about the Wicked Witch?

SABRINA: You mean switch roles with Stacy? Al!

ALLISON: It's for the good of the show, Sabs. It's the professional thing to do.

SABRINA: But how do you know Stacy could pull it off? She doesn't know Dorothy's part either!

ALLISON: She's been at rehearsals, and I've seen her going over the script. I'll bet she could do it. She doesn't have any of your responsibilities.

She could just put all her time into
getting the part right.

(Sabrina thinks for a moment.)

ALLISON: Sabrina? You still there?

SABRINA: I'm here. I really hate to say this,
Al, but I guess you're right.

ALLISON: Good for you, Sabs! I knew you
were a pro! Besides, you'd make a
great Witch. You know you're a
thousand times better actress than
Stacy. It takes a really great actress
to play the Witch convincingly.
Even with all that makeup, Stacy
could never pull it off.

SABRINA: Yeah, well . . . I still want to play
Dorothy.

ALLISON: Someday you will. Right now,
though, you're doing the right
thing, Sabs. I'm proud of you.

SABRINA: Thanks, Al. I guess I better call
Stacy and get it over with.

ALLISON: Good luck.

SABRINA: Thanks, Al. Bye.

ALLISON: Bye.

Sabrina calls Stacy.

MR.
HANSEN: Yes? Hello?
SABRINA: Uh . . . Mr. Hansen? This is Sabrina
            Wells.
MR.
HANSEN: Too bad about the show last night,
            Sabrina. But I'm told a bad dress
            rehearsal means a great opening
            night!
SABRINA: Thanks, Mr. Hansen. Can I talk to
            Stacy, please?
MR.
HANSEN: Why certainly, Sabrina. She's right
            here. Stacy! It's Sabrina.
(Stacy picks up the phone.)
STACY: Hello, Sabrina.
SABRINA: Uh, hi, Stacy. Look, I know the
            show didn't go very well last
            night —
STACY: Oh, that's all right. My father and
            the other teachers told me I was
            brilliant as the Witch. I think I
            really have the best part in the
            show, after all.
SABRINA: Well, that's what I was calling you
            about. We have a problem.

STACY: Oh?

SABRINA: Stacy . . . I need a . . . well, a favor
            from you.

STACY: What favor?

SABRINA: I need you to switch parts with
            me. You can play Dorothy, and . . .
            and I'll play the . . . the Witch.

STACY: You want me to play Dorothy?

SABRINA: Do you think you can do it?

(Stacy gets really excited.)

STACY: Oh, yes! That's so great, Sabrina! I
            mean, I'm sorry not to play the
            Witch, but . . .

SABRINA: (Glumly) Yeah, I know. Forget it.
            Just get the lines memorized so we
            can rehearse on Monday. Okay?

STACY: I'll know them backward and for-
            ward!

SABRINA: Great. Just remember to say them
            forward, okay?

STACY: (Laughs.) You got it! See you at
            rehearsal!

SABRINA: Bye, Stacy.

STACY: Bye!

Chapter Thirteen

That weekend I was so tired I didn't think I'd be able to cackle worth anything. In fact, I wasn't sure I'd even have a voice left. But on Monday I couldn't believe the difference in the show.

My friends were right. I had been trying to do too much. When Stacy showed up at rehearsal on Monday, she knew every line perfectly. I showed her where to move during the songs and scenes. She'd been watching me at rehearsals anyway, so she got most of it right the first time.

Part of me was really miserable about giving up the leading role. But on the other hand, the director inside me knew that the show was a lot stronger than it had been before. Since I wasn't trying to do a hundred things at the same time anymore, I could concentrate on what was really happening onstage.

Allison took over all the things I was worried about backstage, and Katie worked on the program and tickets. Randy supervised all the stuff in the tech booth. I felt a lot better. I even got my homework done before midnight every night. That by itself was an improvement!

"I think we've got a real smash on our hands," Mr. Metcalf told me as we set up for the opening performance. "Everybody really knows their stuff."

I couldn't help glowing a little. I mean, I'd worked really hard to get the Witch's part down, and this time I knew all the lines cold. It wasn't a very large part. But it's true, as Allison said, that it needed a real actress playing it. Besides, I got to scream a lot and strut all over the stage. It was very dramatic stuff.

Randy had even worked out different make-up for me than she'd used for Stacy. That night, as she worked on my face backstage, she explained, "Look, with Stacy, nobody'd believe she was a witch unless we made her look like one. But you can do it with your body and the way you talk, Sabs. That's acting talent. So you don't need all this goop."

"Thanks, Ran," I replied, feeling good that

my friends were behind me. "I think it's going to be fine."

"So do I," Katie added, coming into the rehearsal room. "We're all sold out! In fact, I got permission from Mr. Hansen to let people stand at the back, because more people want to see the show than we can seat in the auditorium!"

"Hooray!" I shouted, forgetting about my green makeup. "That is totally awesome!"

"Hey, watch out, Witchie!" Randy laughed. "You're getting green paint all over the room!"

"We've got the props all set up," Allison reported, coming in behind Katie. "And thank goodness we don't have to worry about the pads coming out of the ruby slippers again!"

We all burst out laughing. With Stacy wearing her own shoes, we didn't have to worry about padding. It was a relief to know the shoes wouldn't fall off her feet the way they fell off mine last week. In fact, I realized that I wasn't feeling nervous at all. I was exhausted from all the preparations, but now that I could concentrate on just one or two things, my whole body felt so much more relaxed.

There was a knock at the rehearsal room door. "You decent?" Sam yelled. "I got a request from the press here!"

Allison, Randy, Katie, and I looked at each other. "The press?" I squeaked out.

Sam came in. "Yeah. Seems the local paper wants a feature interview with the newest and youngest director in Acorn Falls. They want to talk to you right after the show, Sabs, and have you pose for pictures that they can run in Sunday's paper!"

"Wow!" Katie gasped. "You're going to be a real celebrity, Sabs!"

"A true Acorn Falls hero," Randy agreed. She packed up her makeup kit and winked at me. "See? They're never interested in the star of the show, just the director."

"Absolutely," Allison said. "The star is nothing next to the director!"

"That's a fact." Katie laughed. She pulled a program from behind her back. "Anyone want to see what the billing looks like?"

Katie is so cool! The first page of the program read: "Bradley Junior High School's Production of The Wizard of Oz Produced and Directed by Sabrina Wells." My name was in the largest letters next to the title!

"This is awesome!" I exclaimed.

"Everybody'll know who really got the show on!" Allison reminded me. "You're the one who really counts here!"

They all made me feel a lot better. Since Stacy got the part of Dorothy, she'd been telling everyone at rehearsals how she was stepping in to 'save' the show. "I felt sorry for Sabrina," I heard her say during the last rehearsals. "So I offered to help her out. Poor thing, she's just too overwhelmed to play Dorothy."

I was furious at the time, but I also knew that I couldn't get mad. Stacy wasn't the professional that I was. Naturally, she went around bragging all over the place. Besides, it was part of her nature to brag. I didn't think she'd exactly reform now.

"We're ready!" Mr. Metcalf called, coming into the room.

"How's the house?" I asked in my most professional tone. That's how you ask whether anybody's come to see it.

"We're full," he assured me. "People are standing in the aisles — literally! And they all seem very excited."

"Are we ready?" I asked everyone else.

"You call it, Sabrina," Mr. Metcalf told me.

"You're the director."

I loved hearing this, but I told myself to concentrate. "Five minutes from now," I said finally. "Everybody get to your places. Al, call the players for the first scene."

"Right, Sabs," Allison said. Just before she disappeared, she whispered, "Break a leg!"

"Thanks!" I said, waving to her. I felt suddenly like I could move mountains if I had to. I just felt totally confident!

"I'll get to the lighting board," Randy said.

"And I'll go out front," Katie added. "You can be really proud of yourself, Sabs! You've done a great job!"

"If I wasn't wearing all this green stuff, I'd hug you both," I told them, laughing.

"Save it for after the show," Randy advised me. "You're going to be sensational!"

At the end of five minutes I heard the band strike up the overture. Stacy was dressed in Dorothy's checked outfit, waiting with Fluffy in her arms. She looked really nervous. "Good luck, Stacy," I whispered. "Break a leg!"

"Thanks," she replied. I smiled at her. I really did want her to be great tonight. If she wasn't, it would ruin my show. Still, it hardly seemed fair that Stacy would be onstage for most of the time, while I only got to come out for a few short scenes. I reminded myself that this was what being a professional was all about, learning to live with not always being in the spotlight.

I didn't even come on until Munchkinland. As they got close to that scene, I got ready for my entrance. I could hear the audience applauding and laughing at all the funny lines. It was all working great, so far!

The Munchkins were singing and dancing "Ding! Dong! The Witch Is Dead!" when I ran onstage behind a big puff of smoke. I couldn't believe it! I was so made up and looked so mean that the audience started to applaud. And I hadn't said a word yet!

As the applause died away, I advanced on Stacy, trying to look as menacing as possible. "Who killed my sister?" I demanded in my loudest, harshest voice. "Who killed the Witch of the East? Was it you?" I stuck my finger in Stacy's face.

I couldn't believe it. We'd just started the scene, and yet people thought I was so rotten that they were applauding again! This was turning out to be better than I'd ever hoped!

"No," Stacy said in a frightened voice. "It was an accident. I didn't mean to kill anybody."

"Well, my little pretty, I can cause accidents, too!" I rasped. I was really getting into it.

I exited in another big puff of smoke, which got another round of applause from the audience. "I can't believe it!" I whispered to Allison backstage.

"It's a great part, Sabs," she whispered back. "How could they not be crazy about you?"

"But I'm supposed to be rotten!" I protested.

"They know you're just acting," she insisted. "You're just doing a super job!"

Everyone was doing a super job, in fact. The boys had all settled down a lot, so when they danced with Stacy in "We're Off to See the Wizard," nobody bounced and nobody shuffled. They all moved in perfect rhythm. The band was coming in right on cue, with Mr. Metcalf directing them. The lights and sound were exactly the way we'd worked them out to be. It was a four-star, gold-plated opening night!

Before you knew it, we were coming to the big climax scene in the Witch's castle, when the Scarecrow, the Tin Man, and the Lion break in to try to save Dorothy. I chased them around and finally cornered them in the tower. Nobody in the audience was even breathing when I started toward the Scarecrow.

"The last to go" — I pointed to Dorothy — "will see the first three go before her. And her little dog, too!" I whipped my hand behind my back, coming up with a lighted ball. "How about a little fire, Scarecrow?"

I threw the ball toward Rich, and he was supposed to hop around, his back to the audience, so they wouldn't see that he wasn't on fire. But we thought it was perfectly okay to use a real bucket of water to throw at the Witch. And I didn't mind getting wet. In fact, after being under those hot lights, I kind of welcomed the thought. Maybe it would cool me off a little!

Stacy ran forward to the bucket and grabbed it. But for some reason, it must have been filled too full. She had trouble holding on to it, and before you knew it, Fluffy fell to the floor and Stacy had spilled the whole bucket all over herself!

I couldn't believe it! Stacy was drenched from head to foot. And the Scarecrow was still supposed to be on fire! Rich saw what was happening, and quickly plunged his hand into the bucket, pretending to quench the fire that way. Then he picked up the bucket and threw it at me.

Naturally, I stayed dry as a bone. Stacy'd used up all the water in her little accident. But I pretended to be hit and to melt. I was really proud of my melting. I sort of swayed back and forth, all my bones going limp, before I sank to the stage. I got another big round of applause for that.

The rest of the play went fine, although Fluffy refused to go back onstage after that. Still, the audience cheered like crazy when Stacy said her final line, "There's no place like home." Allison closed the curtains, then rolled them back so we could take our bows. Everybody got a huge hand. And when I walked out on the stage, I honestly couldn't believe it! The audience was standing up and screaming! A real standing ovation for me! And then Allison brought out a big bouquet for me from the whole cast. It was the biggest thrill of my whole life!

As I watched the curtain rolling back again

and again, I realized it had all worked out even better than I'd hoped. Stacy was still looking a little damp, but even she had come to realize that the drama club was a good idea. And even though I didn't get the biggest part, I was the one getting the biggest hand . . . and all the publicity in the Sunday paper!

Don't Miss
GIRL TALK #29
FAMILY RULES

"Randy Zak! Where in the world have you been?" my mother shouted at me from the doorway as I skateboarded up the walk to our house. "Do you know what time it is?"

I reached the steps at the front door and hopped off my board. "Um — I don't know," I admitted with a shrug. "I lost my watch."

"It's twenty-three minutes past eleven," she said, sounding like that recording you call to find out the exact time. M — which is what I call my Mom — was more upset with me then I had ever seen her. I wondered what I had done to make her so angry.

Okay, it was Tuesday, a school night, and I had sort of lost track of time and stayed out later than usual. But after all, we lived in Acorn Falls, Minnesota. M was acting like something horrendous happened to me, as if we still lived in the middle of New York City.

Just as I got inside and closed the door, the phone rang. M walked toward the kitchen to get the phone.

"Guess I'll go to bed now," I called after her. "I'm pretty tired."

"Wait right there, please," she said. "We have some more talking to do."

I sighed.

"She just came in," I heard M say, talking about me I guessed. "Oh yes, she's fine. Thanks for calling, Elizabeth." Then I knew M was talking to my friend Allison Cloud's mom.

"Listen, M, I know I'm home a little later than usual," I began to explain, "But honestly, what's the big deal?"

"What's the big deal?" M echoed. "You told me you were going over to Allison's house after school to study for a math test. You left the Cloud's house at five-thirty. It is now almost six hours later and no one had any idea where you were."

Now I was starting to feel a little uncomfortable. You know how sometimes you're in the middle of something and you get this feeling that if you make one wrong move you're going to be in deep trouble? Only you don't know what's the right move, or what's the wrong move? That was exactly how I felt.

TALK BACK!
TELL US WHAT YOU THINK ABOUT
GIRL TALK BOOKS

Name _____

Address _____

City _____ State _____ Zip_____

Birth   Day _____ Mo._____ Year _____

Telephone Number (____)_____

1) Did you like this GIRL TALK book?

Check one: YES_____ NO_____

2) Would you buy another Girl Talk book?

Check one: YES_____ NO_____

If you like GIRL TALK books, please answer questions 3-5;
otherwise go directly to question 6

3) What do you like most about GIRL TALK books?

Check one: Characters_____ Situations_____
        Telephone Talk_____Other_____

4) Who is your favorite GIRL TALK character?

Check one: Sabrina_____ Katie_____ Randy_____
Allison_____ Stacy_____ Other (give name) _____

5) Who is your least favorite character?

_____

6) Where did you buy this GIRL TALK book?

Check one: Book store____Toy store____Discount store____
Grocery store___Supermarket___Other (give name)_____

Please turn over to continue survey.

7) How many GIRL TALK books have you read?

Check one: 0____   1 to 2____   3 to 4 ____   5 or more____

8) In what type of store would you look for GIRL TALK books?

Book store_____Toy store_____Discount store_____

Grocery store_____Supermarket_____Other (give name)_____

9) Which type of store you would visit most often if you wanted to buy a GIRL TALK book.

Check only one: Book store_____Toy store_____

Discount store_____Grocery store_____Supermarket_____

Other (give name)_____

10) How many books do you read in a month?

Check one: 0____   1 to 2____   3 to 4 ____   5 or more____

11) Do you read any of these books?

Check those you have read:

The Babysitters Club_____   Nancy Drew_____

Pen Pals_____   Sweet Valley High _____

Sweet Valley Twins_____Gymnasts_____

12) Where do you shop most often to buy these books?

Check one: Book store_____Toy store_____

Discount store_____Grocery store_____Supermarket_____

Other (give name)_____

13) What other kinds of books do you read most often?

_____

14) What would you like to read more about in GIRL TALK?

_____

_____

Send completed form to :
GIRL TALK Survey Western Publishing Company, Inc.
1220 Mound Avenue, Mail Station #85
Racine, Wisconsin 53404 Survey 3

**LOOK FOR THE AWESOME GIRL TALK BOOKS IN
A STORE NEAR YOU!**